'Simply addictive … It isn't painted as a sixth sense or a mystical ability but does come across as Chastity being very much in her element in those mean streets as the late drinkers head home and the litter blows down the Reeperbahn. Simply an excellent slice of atmospheric crime. Give me more, soon!' Blue Book Balloon

'This novel is steeped in pure grit and darkness. For me the grittiest element was Chastity Riley – a hard-drinking, smoking, no-nonsense, kick-ass prosecutor not afraid to challenge the good and the bad guys … The novel is dark, subversive and just that little bit different from everything in the crime genre' My Bookish Blogspot

'A deliciously dark novel with layers upon layers of mystery, not all uncovered by the end of it. Buchholz leaves her readers intrigued to know more about these characters. Whatever case Chastity Riley takes up next, if indeed she does, I'll be very keen to uncover it with her. The magic of Orenda Books strikes again!' Segnalibro

'Simone Buchholz has created a contemporary thriller with all the coolness of classic Noir. Dark, pessimistic and gritty; exuding atmosphere, the story enveloped me like wisps of cigarette smoke. I loved it and can't wait to read more of this exciting series' Hair Past a Freckle

'The sentences were snappy and the writing was highly addictive and engaging … German Noir is something new to me, but I was utterly enthralled and will most definitely be reading more. Simone Buchholz has a refreshing writing style and a unique talent for drawing the reader right into the heart of the story with the wonderful descriptions of Hamburg and a narrative that is spectacular. Really recommend it' Reflections of a Reader

'The wonderful way that Buchholz brings her plot alive through gritty, punchy and thrilling writing makes this a gripping read that readers can race through, devouring every last, tantalising detail' The Quiet Knitter

'Simone Buchholz has created a striking, thrilling set of characters. With its unique chapters, wonderful writing and show-stopping protagonist, a book that will win over the hearts and minds of a lot of readers! Fast-paced. Dark. Thrilling' Ronnie Turner

'I was kept on my toes with this dark and gritty crime story. It's not a long book but it's certainly packed to the brim and could easily be read in one sitting, it pulls you in, and with relatively short chapters it was very easy to get lost in the story' It's All about the Books

'Sharply written with a staccato sense to it that really draws you in … I loved the character of Chastity, who is cleverly drawn. Overall *Blue Night* is fast, considered and written beautifully. Very different. I like different. It's refreshing. Highly recommended' Liz Loves Books

'Gripping, ominous and delightfully edgy. I can't wait to meet up with Chastity Riley again soon. For a shorter than average novel, it really packs one heck of a punch!' Damppebbles

'A really unique read, and I grew to love the structure and style. Beautifully written and seamlessly translated, Buchholz offers something refreshingly different to what's on the market currently. I urge you to check it out' Bloomin' Brilliant Books

'It has all the danger, thrills and twists required to keep the reader on edge throughout, and I highly recommend it to all crime readers. It was a treat to experience Chastity Riley's story and I hope to cross paths with her again soon' Always Trust in Books

'This story is so atmospheric, and it has done an excellent job of portraying the gritty, raw, seedy hedonism of Hamburg at that time' Sissi Reads

'Buchholz has created a phenomenal female character, Chastity Riley … I found myself racing through each page, eager to find out more … I can't wait to read more from this author' Compulsive Readers

'The chapters are short, which helped to keep the story fresh and made me want to read more … a different and intriguing crime story, and I will be interested in seeing what is in store for Chastity next' Rae Reads

'This is straight up one of the most intriguing books I've had the pleasure of reading! … I imagine it's going to be a long time before I read something quite so extraordinary' The P Turners' Book Blog

'This is a dark, gritty read with heaps of action … it packs a real punch and is a testament to Simone Buchholz's writing … Wonderful' Beverley Has Read

'The chapters are short and are infused with one-liners and monologues, making it a very fast book to read … It is, I imagine, what would have been termed hard-boiled crime fiction, a style synonymous with 1920s America, but with a very modern and German twist' Swirl and Thread

'It's gritty and yes, it's dark but it's also an incredibly refreshing take on the crime-fiction genre with a fabulous cast of characters and a delicious sense of humour that won me over within the first few pages' Novel Deelights

BETON ROUGE

ABOUT THE AUTHOR

Simone Buchholz was born in Hanau in 1972. At university, she studied philosophy and literature, worked as a waitress and a columnist, and trained to be a journalist at the prestigious Henri-Nannen-School in Hamburg. In 2016, Simone Buchholz was awarded the Crime Cologne Award as well as second place in the German Crime Fiction Prize for *Blue Night*, which was number one on the KrimiZEIT Best of Crime List for months. She has also won the Radio Bremen Crime Award and the Crime Prize for the Best Economic Crime Novel. She lives in Sankt Pauli, in the heart of Hamburg, with her husband and son.

Follow Simone on Twitter *@ohneKlippo* and visit her website: *simonebuchholz.com*.

ABOUT THE TRANSLATOR

Rachel Ward is a freelance translator of literary and creative texts from German and French to English. Having studied modern languages at the University of East Anglia, she went on to complete UEA's MA in Literary Translation. Her published translations include *Traitor* by Gudrun Pausewang and *Red Rage* by Brigitte Blobel. Rachel is a Member of the Institute of Translation and Interpreting.

Follow Rachel on Twitter *@FwdTranslations*, on her blog *www. adiscounttickettoeverywhere.wordpress.com*, and on her website: *www. forwardtranslations.co.uk*.

BETON ROUGE

SIMONE BUCHHOLZ

translated by Rachel Ward

**ORENDA
BOOKS**

Orenda Books
16 Carson Road
West Dulwich
London SE21 8HU
www.orendabooks.co.uk

First published in German by Suhrkamp Verlag AG, Berlin 2017
This edition published in the United Kingdom by Orenda Books 2019
Copyright © Suhrkamp Verlag Berlin 2017
English translation © Rachel Ward 2019

ISBN 978-1-912374-59-5
eISBN 978-1-912374-60-1

Typeset in Garamond by MacGuru Ltd
Printed and bound by CPI Group (UK) Ltd, Croydon CR0 4YY

The translation of this work was supported by a
grant from the Goethe-Institut London

For sales and distribution, please contact
info@orendabooks.co.uk or visit *www.orendabooks.co.uk*.

BETON ROUGE

For Neville Longbottom

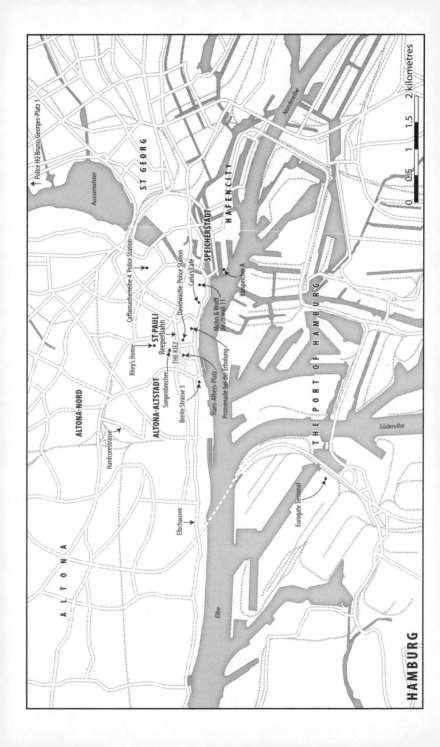

HAMBURG

ALTONA

ALTONA-NORD

ALTONA-ALTSTADT

ST PAULI

ST GEORG

SPEICHERSTADT

HAFEN-CITY

THE PORT OF HAMBURG

Aussenalster

Norderelbe

Süderelbe

Elbe

Hardcorestrasse

Elbchaussee

Riley's Home

Reeperbahn

Sorgenbrecher

THE KIEZ

Breite Strasse 3

Hans-Albers-Platz

Promenade bei der Erholung

Caffamacherreihe 4 Police Station

Davidwache Police Station

Carla's Café

Mohn & Wolff
Brooktwiel 11

Kaispeicher A

Eurogate Terminal

↑ Police HQ Bruno-Georges-Platz 1

0   0.5   1   1.5   2 kilometres

The sky is grey,
The houses are greyer,
A very warm welcome to Grey-upon-Despair,
Eyes scream at me: 'You're not from round here,'
Little red-brick houses, gardens all cement,
For each of life's problem there's an alcoholic drink,
While all of life's joys step over the brink,
Walk through the streets, there's no colour and no life,
The cold social wind cuts right through me like a knife,
See, here, my son, there's no happy ending,
Without immigration, there's not enough befriending,
I'm stranded here like a shipwrecked sailor,
Who doesn't even have enough weed to roll a spliff.

Absolute Beginner: 'Nach Hause' [Going Home]
(from the album 'Advanced Chemistry', 2016)

DOG EAT DOG WORLD

The rain creates walls in the night. Falling from the sky, they are like mirrors, reflecting and warping the blue light from the police car.

Everything spins.

The street emerges from the darkness and loses itself between the harbour lights, and there – right in the middle, just where it suddenly drops downhill – is where it happened: a cyclist.

She's lying, twisted, on the asphalt, her strawberry-blonde hair forming a delicate pool around her head. Her pale dress is awash with blood; the blood seems to be flowing from her side, staining the concrete red. There's a black shoe – some kind of ballet flat – on her right foot and no skin at all on her left. The bike's lying a few feet away on a grass verge, as if it's been ditched.

The woman isn't moving; only her ribcage twitches desperately, as if to rise and fall, but then it doesn't move at all. Her body is trying to take in air from somewhere.

Two paramedics are leaning over and talking to her, but it doesn't look as though they're getting through. It doesn't look as though anything's getting through any more. Death is about to give her a ride.

Two police officers are cordoning off the accident site, shadows dancing on their faces. Now and then, a car comes past and drives slowly around her. The people in the cars don't want to look too closely.

The paramedics do things to their paramedic cases; then they close them, stand up.

That must be it, then.

So, thinks God, looking industrious, that's that. He picks up his well-chewed pencil, crosses the cyclist off, and wonders whose life he could play football with next.

I think: I'm not on duty. I'm just on my way to the nearest pub.

But as I'm here.

'Hello,' I say.

What else was I supposed to say?

'Move along, please,' says the more solid of the two policemen. He's pulled his cap right down over his face; raindrops are glittering on his black moustache. The other has his back to me and is on his phone.

'I certainly can,' I say, 'or I can stay and take care of a few things.' I hold out my hand. 'Chastity Riley, public prosecutor.'

'Ah, OK.'

He takes my hand but doesn't shake it. I feel as though he's holding it. Because that's what you do at times like this, when someone's just died – because a tiny bit of all of us dies along with them and so everything's a bit shaky. The big policeman and I seem suddenly involved in a relationship of mutual uncertainty.

'Dirk Kammann,' he says. 'Davidwache Station. My colleague's on the phone to our CID.'

'OK,' I say.

'OK,' he says, letting go of my hand.

'Hit-and-run?' I ask.

'Looks like it. She hardly drove over her own belly.'

I nod, he nods; we stop talking but stand side by side a while longer. When the dark-blue saloon draws up with the CID guys from the Davidwache, I say goodbye and go, but I look back round before turning the corner. There's a grey veil over the brightly lit scene, and it's not the rain; for once it's not even the persistent rain that falls in my head. This isn't my personal charcoal grey; it's a universal one.

I call Klatsche and tell him that there's nothing doing tonight. That I don't feel like the pub.

Then I go home, sit by the window and stare into the night.

The moon looks like it feels sick.

SHADOWRUNNER

It makes him look so ridiculous. 'Cos he's shit-scared.

First I undressed him, then I strapped him down.

He doesn't like it, of course. Nobody would. He'd rather know the meaning of all this. Keeps asking. He's been asking constantly since he woke up half an hour ago.

But I don't tell him.

You don't always have to know the meaning of all this: the stick in my hands, the Bunsen burner, the saw.

First there's another big dose of chloroform to keep things quiet. Stop the moaning etc.

Then we'll take it from there.

SPECIALIST IN DARK HOLES

Haze lies over the city; last night's rain left it behind. It's too warm, almost twenty degrees this morning, even though it's late September.

I stand on my balcony and drink coffee with this laundry room all around me. The cranes on the horizon have vanished – the thick air's eaten them up. The shrieking of the harbour gulls sounds unusually clear, and almost too close, as if they might put aside their friendliness any minute and start pecking at someone's forehead – maybe mine.

It's just after nine. I ought to go to work.

Go on, then.

I put my coffee – half-gone-cold, half-got-lost – down in the kitchen, take a thin leather jacket from the coat hook, just in case, and set off.

Breathing this haze, which seems to soak up the big-city smog like a sponge, is a bit like smoking. I also light a cigarette – double poisoning is more reliable. I've smoked far too little in the last few days; that needs to change, and so does everything else.

On my third drag, my mobile rings; I answer reluctantly: 'Riley.'

'Good morning, Ms Riley. Kolb here.'

The attorney general. She likes me. And she doesn't like me. It's hit-and-miss. You never quite know.

'Dr Kolb, good morning. What's up?'

'I've got something for you.'

I keep walking through the cloud that's fallen from heaven and find myself thinking about last night's accident. Or, to be precise, I can't stop thinking about last night's accident.

'A hit-and-run?' I ask.

'No. Why do you say that?'

'Just wondered,' I say, drag on my cigarette again and throw it away. Sometimes I'm included in current stuff, sometimes not. I wonder what she wants.

'Where are you now?' she asks.

'On my way to the office.'

'On foot?'

'As ever.'

'In that case, could you please turn right, as unbureaucratically as possible, and head for the harbour?' she says. 'Outside Mohn & Wolff there's a man in a cage, right by the main entrance. The people from the local station are trying to get him out.'

I stop. 'A man in a cage?'

'That's all I know,' she says, and she sounds impatient. 'It's still very fresh. Inspector Stepanovic from SCO 44 called me – presumably they're taking the case. He's on his way, but he's stuck in traffic so he'll be a while. In the meantime, go and take a look, please; it could be a matter of public interest, which could get political.'

I nod and hang up, forgetting, as I so often do, that you can't hear a nod down the phone. But Dr Kolb isn't the kind of person who cares about niceties. Perhaps that's one of the main things we have in common.

A man in a cage outside Hamburg's biggest magazine publisher. For the moment, it sounds more like really weird guerrilla marketing than anything 'political'. 'Political' can only mean one of two things:

1. Something's happened and people might take to the barricades, so the mayor's busy getting his best troops together.
2. We don't know if there's anything funny about this, so we're keeping things quiet for the moment, but in public we want it to look like we're being totally transparent and totally on it and generally the total dog's bollocks.

In scenario one, I don't figure – I'm not one of the mayor's best people, I'm one of his best-hidden people. So it boils down to scenario two – in which Riley, specialist in dark holes, gets let out of her own dark hole.

I'm intrigued that someone from Serious Crime Office 44 is on the way. I'm still not sure exactly what their area is. But they're some kind of hardcore guys, I know that. So much for we're totally on it and totally awesome.

We'll see about that.

I step on it and break into a run, heading for the Bismarck monument.

SPAT ON

The cage is made of black metal. It has thick, extremely robust-looking bars, and it's not particularly big. Just large enough for a grown man to fit inside if you fold him in half first. The man is about forty, maybe even forty-five, it's hard to say for sure. He's very thin and in pretty good shape, and his features are perfectly formed. His dark hair is cut short at the back and sides, but just a fraction over-long on top; strands fall onto his face. Combed back, the style demands a suit. But at the moment, the man is naked and injured and so far out of his senses that it's hard for my mind to sustain the businesslike image of the guy that it's built up without my even thinking about it. He has welts on his wrists and ankles, as if he's spent quite a while tied up. His whole body is covered with livid bruises and scratches. And, as if I'm looking at a bloody, weeping painting, somehow I get a sense of something very much like despair – but I can't say where the despair is coming from: from the man who's been stuffed in the cage like a rabid animal, or from the person who's done it. What I'm looking at seems to depict a complete absence of voluntary action.

I have to take a deep breath, and then another and another, before I can move a few steps closer.

It looks as though the naked man's consciousness is now working its way, bit by bit, to the surface. His eyes are closed and he's slowly moving his head to and fro while one of the two uniformed police-men tortures the padlock on the cage with a bolt cutter – it's obviously putting up quite a fight. It's a pretty impressive padlock – it's about the size of a small loaf of bread and it looks a couple of hundred years old. The cage has been placed right outside the main entrance to the building. If you want to go through the revolving glass door, you have to pass the cage. Seen from the harbour, the massive glass façade resembles a gigantic cruise ship; now it's reflecting the sun, which is pushing through the clouds in perfect time with the man in the cage coming round.

A sprinkling of onlookers stands round the cage. Some are smoking, and judging by their coolness and unobtrusively elegant clothes, a few are journalists. OK, they're running a bit late, but they can't just walk past this confusing arrangement on their way to work. The majority look more like tourists – part of the horde that the harbour disgorges every morning. They're wearing little rucksacks, cropped trousers and practical jackets. It always strikes me that tourists in Hamburg look completely different from tourists in Munich or Berlin, where it wouldn't occur to anybody to stick a sou'wester on their head. Some even have those mad, modern walking sticks. Perhaps they think Hamburg is already on the North Sea, although that's a good thirty to fifty years off yet. It freaks me out that some people plan so far in advance, even if it's only for one holiday. I prefer to take things as they come.

'Morning,' I say, coming to stand beside the two policemen.

'Morning, Ms Riley,' says the one standing up, who either wants to leave the other guy to get on with it or is simply above such a task. We must have met, seeing as he knows my name this early in the morning. He's definitely in his late fifties, has a mighty belly, and there are grey curls on the back of his neck, curling under his uniform cap. The name on his police jacket reads 'Flotow'. Ah, I remember: Station 16, on Lerchenstrasse.

'We met at Lerchenstrasse,' I say.

'Yeah,' he says. 'Switched six months ago. Station 14, Caffa-macherreihe.' He shoves his hands in his trouser pockets in that passive-aggressive way beloved of fattish, older, not particularly tall men, and looks reproachfully at me. 'I'd had it up to here with the red-light scene in the Kiez.'

As if the Kiez were my responsibility. When it's more like the Kiez is responsible for me.

Sergeant Flotow turns back to his colleague, who's still sweating and cursing over the lock. 'Get a move on, Hoschi. The poor bloke'll wake up soon, and then he'll start screaming at us too.'

Hoschi grunts, and I imagine that it means something like 'get on with it yourself, dickhead', but, unfortunately for Hoschi, the four pale-blue stars on Sergeant Flotow's epaulets make it abundantly clear who's in charge here – and whose job it is to kindly get on with wrestling with the bloody lock.

'Officer Lienen,' says Flotow, pointing at his colleague on the pavement.

'Morning Mr Lienen,' I say, kneeling down beside him.

He's nearly got the lock.

'You've nearly got the lock,' I say, trying to look encouraging. Unfortunately, encouraging looks aren't part of my skillset, so the result is a kind of tic that nobody understands.

Lienen looks at me, his eyes narrowed to slits. His expression conveys such violent contempt for his boss that I think: Hoschi, you and I should go for a beer, preferably right now.

'Exhibiting a person in a cage,' I say. 'That's properly sick.'

'You should have seen what was going on here when we arrived,' says Lienen, shaking his head in a way that's half annoyed and half confused.

'What was going on?'

The padlock gives – *crack* – way and falls apart. Lienen stands up. He holds the bolt cutter like a baseball bat.

'Well,' says Flotow, 'people weren't exactly acting civilised.'

Lienen pushes back his cap and wipes the sweat from his brow.

'Meaning?' I ask.

'They were doing something very unpleasant,' says Flotow.

Aha. Doing something very unpleasant. Do I really have to winkle every detail out of him? I more or less plant myself in front of Flotow.

'Don't make me winkle every detail out of you,' I say. 'What was the situation in the moment you arrived? And what is it now?'

He sucks his teeth, nods in an oh-so-it's-like-that kind of way, straightens his trousers without taking his hands out of his pockets, which leaves them pulled up much too high, then rocks to and fro on his toes and looks at me like I'm a badly brought-up child. I look back as truculently as possible, and because he can't decide on the spot which of us is stronger, he decides not to let it come to that.

'The woman at reception rang us,' he says. 'That was about half past eight. She said something about an unpleasant crowd of people outside the building. And that she thought someone was in danger. But she wouldn't be more precise, not even when pressed.'

Lienen kneels in front of the cage again and tries to cover the naked man with one of those gold thermal blankets.

'And then?' I ask.

'We set off,' says Flotow.

He still has his hands in his trouser pockets, and he's still trying to run me aground.

But he thinks better of it.

'There were about fifty people,' he says. 'They were just standing there. And some of them – I literally had to look twice because I couldn't believe it – they were spitting at the cage. When we pulled up in the patrol car, they went into the building.'

You were lucky, old man.

'It was dead quiet,' says Lienen, 'and they were spitting. It was creepy.' He doesn't look at me – keeps his eyes on the man in the golden cape. 'I've never seen anything like it. It felt like it could escalate at any minute. They looked like predators, just before they fall on their prey. They weren't even taking photos, and people take photos of everything these days. They really were just standing there, spitting, and working the poor bloke over with their eyes.'

'Were you able to get their details?' I ask.

'A few of them,' says Lienen. 'But there were too many, and they hurried away and vanished inside.' He nods towards the glass façade.

'The place is massive. And there were only two of us. The CID guys are here now, in the foyer, still trying to pin a few people down.'

He twitches the foil blanket straight. The things are so damn slippery that a bit of the person the foil's meant to be protecting is always left sticking out.

'And somebody had to call an ambulance first,' he says.

'True,' I say. 'Where's it got to, anyway?'

The man in the cage is starting to move. He puts his left hand to his face and tries to support himself on his right. The gold foil slips. Lienen speaks softly to him.

'Call them again, please,' I say to Flotow, then I kneel in front of the cage next to Lienen.

The man opens his eyes and glances enquiringly at us: Am I dead?

Bottom left, at the foot of the steps, a brown Mercedes races into my field of vision. The driver spins the tyres with a screech, then he stops, gets out, stretches somewhat awkwardly and climbs the steps just as fast as he drove up.

CAN'T YET QUITE BE CLASSIFED

'Ivo Stepanovic,' says my new colleague, holding out his hand. 'SCO 44.'

'Chastity Riley,' I say, looking up at him. 'Public prosecutor.' Wow, he's tall.

'Sorry – Cassidy?'

'Never mind.'

'Come on, tell me your name again. I didn't quite catch it.'

His expression is on the borderline between annoyed and interested. But also 'let's not start off like this, doll'.

'Call me Riley.'

'OK, Riley, you can call me Stepi.'

'Stepi?'

'Joke.' He purses his lips and wrinkles his brow, shoves his hands in his trouser pockets and looks around.

So this is him, the guy from the 44s, our funky specialist squad – the ladies and gentlemen of serious crime, although I've never heard of a woman working there. The 44s are concerned with jewel thefts and bank robberies, hostage situations and major league blackmail, and any kind of situation that can't yet quite be classified. Something new or particularly puzzling. Something like a naked man in a cage. Something like me, maybe.

Stepanovic is wearing a somewhat crumpled black shirt that isn't quite straining over his belly but might be soon, plus jeans and black ankle boots. His thick, greying hair is cut short; his nose looks as though it's been broken more like three times than twice; his dark designer stubble is clipped but very dense, his eyebrows have class, his eyes gleam an indefinable shade – I'd guess at mud. Furrows traverse his skin, but they're in the right places: at the corners of his eyes, on his forehead – a few each side of his mouth. His handshake just now was a fraction short of vicelike. An almost good-looking and extremely opaque guy.

Right now, I don't quite know what to make of him.

But then I don't quite know what to make of most people for the first two or three years after we've met.

He blinks in the thin sunlight, takes a deep breath, turns his head once to the left and once to the right; I hear a crack, and he groans slightly. Had a long night, I'm guessing.

'So,' he says, 'shall we?'

If I'm not very much mistaken, I can hear the slightest hint of a Frankfurt accent, but I try not to take that seriously.

Stepanovic turns to the guys from the station; Officer Lienen has now helped the naked man in foil out of the cage. The man is leaning against a wall, half sitting, half lying, trying to open his eyes; and whenever he finally manages it, he's trying to keep them open. He can't do it. Lienen has crouched down beside him and is speaking quietly to him again. Stepanovic shakes hands with Flotow and nods carefully towards Lienen, as if to say, I don't want to interrupt; we'll say hello later.

Then he takes two, three big steps back and does something that I've often seen Faller and Calabretta do, but never with this intensity: he looks over the crime scene as if seeing it through a camera.

He starts with the long shot. His gaze rests on the scene for at least two minutes. Then he turns slowly on his own axis, presumably memorising the possible access, escape and transport routes. Finally, he gets to work on the details.

The cage.

The padlock.

The victim.

Zooms in very close on everything.

'I need photos,' he says to Flotow.

Who nods, officiously. 'Right away, boss.'

He seems all-round impressed and ready to kiss up.

Stepanovic raises his hands and plays it down: relax. He comes over to me.

'What kind of perverted stunt is this with the cage? Have you ever seen anything like it?'

I shake my head.

He joins in.

'Where'd it come from, I wonder?' he asks. 'The circus?'

'Definitely looks like something to do with animals,' I say.

'Weird,' he says. 'Could you briefly fill me in on what's happened so far?'

'I certainly can,' I say, 'but the other two were here first.'

'Oh,' he says, 'never mind that.' Waves his hand. 'They're busy. Can't be bothered with answering my questions just now. I'll get round a table with everyone later. If you can just bring me up to speed now, we'll go inside. I want to know what's going on in there.'

He looks over the outside of the building while I tell him what I know.

Meanwhile I look over his outsides.

So, I'm meant to work with this guy now.

Got it.

THE MAIN THING IS TO KEEP THE FRONT GARDEN IMMACULATE

Two women and two men from CID are standing in the foyer, which in some subliminal way manages to feel depressing. If the building looks like a ship from the outside, from the inside it looks like an engine room. Corridors and staircases lead off all over the place, the glass façade is reinforced by steel ribs, the ceiling hangs low and dark over our heads.

A cluster of black leather armchairs stands listlessly to the left of the entrance. Around twenty people are sitting in them; just by looking at them you can tell that they were asked to stay right there. None of them are relaxed; they're all as stiff as broccoli. The CID officers are writing things in their notebooks. Now and again, questions are being asked – more and more of them, with the police quizzing the journalists, which the journalists must feel is like an inside-out press conference. At any rate, their faces say: what *is* this shit?

It's amazing how similar the reporters and the detectives are, at least in terms of their clothes and attitude. The only fundamental difference between the two groups is their jackets: for the CID teams it's jeans and T-shirt with a tight leather jacket, while the gutter press opts for an ultra-reserved blazer or well-cut corduroy. I look down at myself, at the thin, brown leather jacket in my hand, which I seem to have been lugging around with me for about twenty years, and think, yet again, that I'd definitely have passed muster as a policewoman.

Stepanovic goes over to his colleagues, briefly introduces himself and points to me, then he nods and holds his right hand to his ear, sign language for 'I'll call you'. His colleagues nod in return, but he's already turned his back on them. Three big strides bring him to me, and two more take him to the lady at reception.

'Stepanovic, Hamburg Serious Crime Office,' he says, holding his ID under her nose. 'And this is Ms Riley from the Public Prosecution Service.'

The little mouse of a receptionist is blonde, pretty, delicate and still a long way off thirty. Little bun at the nape of her neck; bright-green cotton cardigan around her shoulders. Not the kind of woman to lead the way. In three to four years, she'll be assistant to the editor-in-chief of a second-rate magazine, and the editor-in-chief will be a man. Shortly afterwards, she'll marry that man's deputy, move to the suburbs and have two children, who'll be even prettier than she is. By then, her husband will have become editor-in-chief of whatever magazine and everything in the front garden at home will be kept immaculate, and that's the main thing.

I always wonder how anyone can stand a life like that, where colouring over the lines is never, absolutely never, ever permitted. Or if maybe they actually like it like that. At the same time, I wonder why I was born holding a pencil that, when I use it, will only leave any kind of visible mark outside the margins.

Anyway: the mouse on reception was the one who called the police. And she has information for us.

'That's Tobias Rösch over there in that cage,' she says. She points her finger towards the entrance but doesn't look.

'He's out of the cage now,' I say.

'Well, thank God for that. I was starting to feel sorry for him, poor man.'

'Didn't you feel sorry for him at first?' I ask.

She leans a little closer to me and makes a face as if I ought to know what's coming next. 'Mr Rösch is head of HR,' she says quietly.

I suck my teeth and pull my head back a bit, as if to say: Oh, right, I see – an arsehole.

Head of HR is obviously not a role that'll make you popular in a time of crisis. Right now, his main job will be implementing the board's proposed savings in the places they hurt the most. Meaning he's probably meant to be getting rid of as many staff as possible, as quickly and as cheaply as he can, and then replacing them with low-cost freelancers.

'I'd like to speak to the shop steward,' says Stepanovic.

And I think that I'd actually still like to know why the mouse didn't ring the police until around half past eight, by which point a pretty revolting state of affairs had developed round the cage. What time do the first people get here? Around eight? So why didn't anyone ring us right away and say that there was a person lying here?

We'll sort that out later. The CID will sort it out, says my inner guide to official channels. I have to learn to keep out sometimes.

The receptionist pouts and looks a bit miffed, clearly sensing that she might have palled up with us too soon, then favours us with the smile that she's paid to deliver, reaches for the phone and dials a number. She lets it ring. Then she hangs up.

'Mr Grabowski isn't answering. He must be out of his office somewhere.'

Hold that smile.

'We can easily wait for him in his office,' I say.

'I'm afraid I can't leave my desk to take you up,' she says, looking genuinely disappointed. I really wouldn't like to be the man who has to endure this emotional spin cycle.

'All the same,' I say.

'OK.'

Thin lips. All smiled out.

She pulls a slip of paper off a small pad, writes something on it, pushes it over the reception desk and makes her lips thinner still. On the paper it says: 'Robert Grabowski, D 107.'

'Will you find it?'

Governessy look.

Will we find it?

Beats me if we'll find it. Do we look like boy scouts? I mean, we've never been here before and the place is as convoluted as the engine room on a cruise ship. How should we know if we'll find it? Part of me wants to give the receptionist a slap; the other part would rather shove her face in a pan of something sticky. I'm slowly running out of patience with uncooperative conversationalists this morning.

Stepanovic takes the note, pockets it, gives my elbow an unobtrusive tug and says, 'Come on, Riley. We'll find it. I'm a cop, aren't I?'

THE SHIT'S ALWAYS PASSED DOWNWARDS

In Robert Grabowski's office, Stepanovic is sitting on the swivel chair at Grabowski's desk; I'm sitting on the radiator, which is so low, my face is between my knees; it's as if I've borrowed a kid's bike. Stepanovic rolls back and forth on the chair and looks at me.

'What do you reckon? What exactly happened there? Joint effort by the staff?'

'No,' I say. 'This can't be a group thing. This is one guy burning with rage – it's got to be personal. Anyway, journalists usually reach for other weapons, don't they?'

'Words, you mean.'

'Exactly,' I say. 'Words, texts, meetings, publicity, et cetera.' I squirm on the radiator. Bloody uncomfortable spot I've picked. 'All the same, there's got to be a story here – something to do with this place. Or Mr HR wouldn't have been served up on a platter right here.'

'Have you got any cigarettes, by the way?'

'Sure. Haven't you?'

'Left them at home,' he says. 'I was in a bit of a rush this morning.'

Somehow, I don't believe that he came here from home, but that's none of my business. Besides, 'at home' can also mean somewhere private, overnight.

I turn around. Behind me, there's a balcony door and behind the door there's a balcony. Mix and match.

'If we go for a smoke now, the bus will come,' says Stepanovic.

'Robert Grabowski, you mean.'

He grins, looking at me like the boys always looked at me when we were kids, just before we got into some kind of trouble together, me and the guys on the back row.

He stands up and holds out his hand to me. I take it; he pulls me up with a heave.

'Come on, Riley, let's call the bus.'

We go out and light our cigarettes, and just as we take the second drag, which is always the best one, there's Grabowski standing in the office doorway.

'Ahem! Can I help you?'

We probably ought to feel bad right now, and we probably ought to show it; we ought at least to apologise. But Stepanovic just acts as if nothing's happened.

'Mr Grabowski. Nice to see you.'

He takes another drag on his cigarette and throws it overboard. I follow suit.

'Who are you?'

Grabowski puts on an outraged face, but he can only partially hide the fact that he doesn't really give a damn whether strangers are smoking on his balcony or not. I can tell from his grey skin that he'd probably have been glad to join us if we hadn't thrown our cigarettes away so hastily. His hair was probably dark blond once, and maybe it still is, that's not altogether clear. He's wearing a claret-coloured polo shirt, pale trousers and soft, comfortable, lace-up shoes. Typical shop-steward uniform.

Stepanovic walks over to him and holds up his ID again. He always seems to relish that. I bet he also loves reaching through his car's open window to slap a blue light on the roof.

'Ivo Stepanovic, Serious Crime Office,' he says before pointing to me. 'And this is Ms Riley from the Prosecution Service.'

'Hello, Mr Grabowksi,' I say, trying to put on a friendly face. If we can get only a few things right, around now, the situation might just tip in our favour. 'We'd like to speak to you about Tobias Rösch.'

Grabowski crosses his arms and commits himself.

'Tobias Rösch is a slimy little opportunist. Classic case of kiss up and kick down.'

Whoa, there.

'Might that have landed him in the cage he was lying in this morning?' asks Stepanovic. 'You know what happened, don't you?'

'I'm a journalist,' says Grabowski. 'This whole place is full of journalists. Everybody here knows what happened.'

'We, on the other hand, are just starting to get a picture of it,' I say. 'So, what exactly did happen?'

Grabowski still has his arms crossed, but now he's leaning casually against the doorframe.

I'm a journalist.

And this is my office.

'That nice Mr Rösch was lying naked and beaten up in a cage, and nobody was particularly bothered,' he says. 'That's what happened.'

'Two of our colleagues saw Tobias Rösch being spat on by the people standing gawping round the cage,' says Stepanovic.

'That's the first I've heard of it,' says Grabowski, who now seems to fill the doorframe.

'Do you think Rösch deserves to be spat on?' I ask.

Grabowski comes out of his doorframe and walks through his office to his desk. I'm still standing rather more outside than inside. Stepanovic is leaning against Grabowski's file shelves. The shop steward turns his back on me, bends awkwardly, pulls open a desk drawer and reaches for a black leather case. Then he sits down and starts rolling a cigarette.

Once he's dampened the paper with his tongue, he looks at us and says: 'That's a damned leading question.'

Once again, people: I'm a journalist, you're in my office, so play by the rules.

He seals his cigarette, wipes a few tobacco crumbs off his desk and says: 'I don't know whether the same principle applies in your offices, but I imagine it does: the shit's always passed downwards.'

'A fine principle,' says Stepanovic. 'If you're the one sitting at the top.'

Grabowski looks at me.

'There, you see? Your colleague knows what I mean.'

So do I, believe me. It's just that, more often than not, I'm the one who has to take delivery.

Grabowski leans back in his chair, crosses his legs and lights his cigarette. After all, where would we be if the shop steward took any notice of namby-pamby rules such as a ban on smoking in offices?

'The gentlemen on the top floor here are real champion shit-passers,' he says. 'They've spent years making the wrong decisions and sleeping while opportunities pass them by; they abandon titles and chuck new mags and oh-so-innovative ideas into the market in their place at such a rate, you sometimes get the feeling that their first official act every morning must be ramming their heads into the wall, before deciding what will benefit the business and its staff.'

He drags fiercely on his cigarette.

'But that might be giving them way too much credit. There are plenty of people here who see things very differently. They're convinced that the management are only concerned about their own pockets, their own brilliance, and that they're completely oblivious to what happens to the staff. Have you heard the rumour going around here?'

I shake my head and think: No. Have you?

Stepanovic looks at him. Shoot.

'The rumour goes like this: one cosy evening round the fireplace at Villa Wolff on the Elbe, our chief exec did a deal with Mohn & Wolff's major shareholders. If he manages to wind up the firm within the next four years without too much fuss, he'll get a direct flight to the boardroom at the head office in New York, including a penthouse with a view of Central Park.'

'What do you mean, "wind up"?' I ask.

'Break it up,' says Grabowski. 'Sell the magazines off piecemeal to other publishers. The new publisher can replace the editorial staff.

Hire loads of junior editors, for example, and pay them well below the union rate. In return, they get a well-established magazine with plenty of subscribers. That could definitely be lucrative for a smaller firm. And the venerable company of Mohn & Wolff, with its good jobs for good journalists, will no longer exist.'

'Why would the shareholders want that?' I ask.

'Because there's no money in magazines now. Because the profits are shrinking year on year.'

'But it's still going strong, isn't it?' says Stepanovic. 'I just read somewhere that Mohn & Wolff made a profit of almost a hundred million euros last year.'

'That's right,' says Grabowski. 'But that's not enough for them any more.'

THINGS PEOPLE DO WHEN THERE'S TROUBLE

The cage squad has been given a base in a meeting room at Caffa-macherreihe Station – by Hamburg standards, it's relatively bright, but rather small. The room contains precisely four desks. One for Serious Crime, i.e. Stepanovic, and three for the station's CID guys. Small office, small squad.

All the windows are open because it's so warm in this little den, and presumably someone thought it'd be good to get some air; but all that creeps into the room from outside is oppressive damp.

First up, hands are shaken. Sibel Sahin, Bodo Ippig and Daniel Acolatse from Station 14; Ivo Stepanovic from SCO 44.

Chastity Riley, Prosecution Service.

Hello.

Hello, hello, hello.

Detective Superintendent Sahin is about my age, maybe a year or two younger; I'd guess at early forties. She's small and in conspicuously good shape; under her black T-shirt are extremely well-defined shoulders and she has that dangerous sort of body whose sinews and muscles twitch with every movement, no matter how slight. A machine of a woman. Her dark-brown hair is chin length and more or less shoved back behind her ears. Detective Chief Inspectors Ippig and Acolatse aren't exactly spring chickens any more, but they're pretty strapping, too.

Ippig is almost as tall as Stepanovic and similarly broad-shouldered; he has dense, light-brown hair and reddish stubble: a lumberjack shirt kind of guy. He looks rustic yet boyish. Acolatse is a good head shorter; instead of the standard CID jeans, he's wearing slim suit trousers and a dark-blue shirt; very wise, almost black eyes sparkle in his elegant, West African face; his thick hair is cropped to a few millimetres.

I feel that it would be wise to pull Officer Lienen into the squad, but Stepanovic says that he doesn't want any uniformed police on the team.

A little arseholery that I find irritating, but then each to their own.

We push the tables together in the middle, I pull up a fifth chair for myself, we all sit down and Stepanovic explains for a bit how he works – or how he shares out the work.

He's the interrogation expert.

He's the crime-scene expert.

He's the boss.

And the CID works for the boss.

CID representative Sahin's eyebrows shoot up so high that I'm afraid they'll launch off towards the ceiling any minute. Our eyes meet. I try a bit of telepathy: Don't worry, we'll reel him in. It'll happen all by itself once we get down to everyday work. He can't spend the whole time parading his superiority; you don't get anywhere like that. It'll be OK, men always start out this way.

Ippig and Acolatse take it calmly. Plus or minus one boss – whatever. They stand up and start hanging stuff all over the walls.

Pictures of the cage. Pictures of the victim.

Lists of names. Questioned witnesses and witnesses to be questioned. They leave rather too much space beneath the name Tobias Rösch.

It could be coincidence, or they might both share my rotten premonition, I don't know; I'm not good with feelings. But our conversation with Mr Shop Steward has made me think that things are clearly brewing at Mohn & Wolff. And there might be more to come; what, I can't say. I don't want to spread doom and gloom, though, so I keep that thought to myself, put on a face that hints at competence and don't really listen while the others talk among themselves.

Dole out the witness interviews.

Pester SOCO.

Harass forensics to make them tell us something about that uncomfortable cage as soon as possible. Which reminds me: the cage. Acolatse reckons it could have been made for transporting dogs, says his parents once used something like it for their St Bernard when they wanted to fly him to Africa – the dog, that is. You can get them quite easily on the internet, they're not even very expensive: less than a hundred euros. I think about cages for less than a hundred euros, and about what mountain-rescue dogs must feel like when they're flown to some place in a thing like that, and zone out.

So. Make a note of that Riley, won't you? They're doing their job; you do yours. Which means first I trek over to the office to make a start on the charges – against person or persons unknown – of coercion, false imprisonment and grievous bodily harm.

You know, all the things that people do when there's a problem.

Things gulls do: tug at my heart the moment I see them. Who am I kidding? I just need to hear them in the distance, and they've got me. I'm running behind them, scanning the sky, and once I spot them I stand very still, and everything else switches off. All I can do is watch the gulls. God knows why the bastards stir me like that, but they always have. As if they were eternal creatures. I've seen hundreds of dead pigeons. But never a dead gull.

It's only two streets from the station to my office at the Prosecution Service, maybe five minutes' walk. Not a beautiful route: faceless inner-city buildings, some fairly old, some fairly new; as a whole, all totally samey. But up there, now to my left, now leftish, now in the middle, there's music playing; there are the gulls, and one of them even plays at nosediving, but then there it is again, standing against the wind with the others. Three gulls equal a group, and a group turns a route into a stroll.

And if you believe that, you'll believe anything.

WEATHER PHENOMENA

In the evening, shortly before seven, shortly before the climate changes, the evening sun dispenses golden light and it's not even slightly cooler than at midday. I haven't put my leather jacket on once today; it's hanging from my hand, almost a bit insulted. Why take me with you if you don't need me?

The door to the Blue Night is ajar, which, in the Kiez, means something like: there's nothing much going on here yet, but I'm here, feel free to come in if something comes up. Or walk on. Or just do whatever you like.

I go in and hang my insulted jacket on the first chair that comes to hand. The indigo walls gleam in the last rays of the sun, but that's about it for glow. None of the candles and neon signs that light up the Blue Night in the evening are lit yet, and in a moment, when the sun leaves the room, even this bar will just be a joint that smells of last night's booze. Since last spring, when there were three dead men lying in the cellar here, the spark's gone out of this place a bit. It's like a doomed romance: we try desperately to keep it alive by smiling and acting like nothing's wrong, but secretly we're shivering.

Recently, Klatsche talked for the first time about giving up the Blue Night and doing something else. 'Something with an adrenaline rush.'

On my way to the bar, I run my fingers over the tables. Wood never gets properly cold, unlike skin.

Behind the old, solid bar, the cellar hatch is open and out of it shines a beam of light. Down below there's a rumbling and a clattering. Klatsche's busy. Sounds like he's shifting beer crates from side to side.

'Hey!' I call through the hatch.

'Yup!' he calls back.

I climb down the ladder.

It's just as I thought. He's standing in the furthest corner, heaving crates. One night, not all that long ago, we found something very exciting in that very same corner: us. But suddenly, a few nights later, there were three of his former business partners lying there with their faces in the dust and bullets in their heads. Since then, I haven't been very keen on coming down here, even though I repainted the cellar walls with my own hands.

He stops his beer-crate weight training and looks at me. I could bring the evening sun down here. The thing that's filling the room up there. We wouldn't even need to close the bar door. We've always been quick. Fast breeders, Klatsche calls us. But I don't know. I'm not in the mood. And I don't even know why not.

He comes towards me.

'Well, madame?'

'*Moi?*' I ask.

'Uh-huh,' he says. 'How was your day?'

'There was a naked man in a cage.'

'Tricky,' he says. 'What do you want? Beer?'

'Maybe.'

He bends, takes two bottles of Astra from the crate by his feet and pulls his lighter from his trouser pocket. He opens the bottles and presses one into my hand. We drink.

He comes closer, looks at me and lays his hand under my chin.

'Chas?'

'Hm?'

'Either piss off or sleep with me.'

I take his hand from my chin, lay it on his chest, glance briefly at him again and give him a rapid kiss. Then I turn round and piss off, taking my beer with me.

But I must have forgotten the jacket.

JUST AS WELL ALONE

I can't go back to fetch it though.

I could go home and get another.

I could go to the pub closest to my flat and just drink so much that, later, I won't get cold on the short walk home.

Fantastic idea.

I call everyone and ask if they want to come.

No one comes.

Carla is 'having a conversation' with Rocco, whatever that's meant to achieve, and Calabretta doesn't answer. Faller's been on holiday for months, somewhere in Spain. That's all the friends I have.

I could potentially call my colleagues Schulle and Brückner. After all, we've had a few evenings when nothing much mattered in the end; but that was quite a while ago now, and I'd feel a bit sleazy about it.

Hell.

I can drink just as well alone.

BLOOD MOON, BLONDE MOOD

'Looks like it,' I say when the guy asks if the barstool next to me is free.

'Yes,' I say when he asks if he can buy me a schnapps.

'Sure,' I say when he asks if vodka's OK.

We say 'well then' and 'cheers', and when he asks me, after the second vodka, if I've got a reason for getting drunk, I say: 'Not more than usual, actually.'

He smiles to himself as if someone has finally explained the whole damn world to him. I've found my partner for the night. He drinks bottled beer, I drink white wine. Other people have dance partners, I have drinking partners.

He looks good with his ironed shirt and his tousled hair and that thin moustache. I put him at mid-thirties, tops, but his eyes look as though they're made of ancient granite. It's the kind of joke that appeals to me.

He says he's not here to talk though.

I say he's already said plenty for someone who's not here to talk.

The pub door opens and a guy comes in: one of those never-ageing hip hop boys who, even in their early forties, look like they won't finish school until next year. He and the barman clearly know each other well; they grin at each other, point their fingers at each other, do that swaggering, pimp roll thing. And then the hip hop boy says, 'Crack without the pipe, please!' and everyone starts laughing, and then the barman gives him a beer and a rum, and before long there's quite a weight in my drinking partner's gaze. I intercept it and throw it back. Over and over and over again, back and forth it goes.

Then we put the money on the bar. He says he lives just round the corner, I say I don't, and he doesn't care that that was a lie.

In the sky there's that moon that they were talking about on the radio this morning. It's enormous and it's red; it speaks of closeness and distance all at once, and it's shining with all its might on this pavement where I've never lain and will probably never lie. The moon pulls me up to it, I pull the man down to me. His hand below my spine and my hand on the nape of his neck are enough of a go-ahead for us, a flight to the moon and back. Look out, we're flying and we're there, it's over almost as fast as we drank. Undressing really would have been a waste of effort.

Later, we lie half side by side and half on top of each other, and smoke cigarettes.

Perhaps I should have asked him his name.

BLACK BOX ONE

It's not even half past ten and I'm already totally drunk and totally shagged out and sort of on the way home. It's not actually an uncommon scene in this neck of the woods, but at this time of the evening perhaps it is a little unseemly. I walk along every possible side street just to make sure I don't meet anyone I know. Despite all my precautions, though, someone does cross my path, via my telephone. A quiet chirrup: a message from Faller.

A picture.

Some colourful drink.

Then: *Cheers.*

Cheers to you too, I write back, not without making seventy-four typos.

Well, Chas? Where are you hanging out?

Heading home. And you?

Little bar on the beach in Conil.

Conil?

Andalusia. You know.

Course I know. But I was trying to forget.

Then I type: *Text bundle or something?*

Faller never normally sends texts. He says it's too expensive.

It's new, he writes. *What else is up?*

Nothing.

He obviously realises that that's not true but, unlike me, he always knows when to stop. And he can probably tell, even from almost two thousand miles away, that he's caught me out in something.

RESCUED FOR YOU

A knock at my door. I'm lying in bed fully dressed. My head's buzzing. When you drink early, you get hungover early. I squint at my phone: two a.m. Normal midweek closing time at the Blue Night. Stagger to the door, open it, almost pass out on the way, but cling to the wall at the last second. Nicely done, Riley.

Klatsche stands in the doorway. With that Klatschesque air that's unique to him, that nobody else can manage. His whole body says: hey, baby?

But it's not working. Not today, not on me. As if the buttons he can normally press have been disconnected. OK: I was perfectly willing to have them disconnected for me earlier this evening.

He eyes me up. Clocks that something isn't right. He knows what it's like.

'What sorrows were you drowning?'

'Dunno,' I say. 'I drowned 'em.'

'Can I come in?'

'Sure.'

He's got my jacket in his hand.

'Rescued it for you.'

'Thanks,' I say, and the lie falls out of my mouth, squelching unpleasantly as it bursts on the floor.

EXECUTIVES
(FUCK ALL OF YOU)

I've brought too much coffee: Acolatse and Ippig aren't here. So I put two of the cups on the table between Sahin and Stepanovic and take the other two out to reception. Someone who needs coffee will find them.

Meanwhile, my two new colleagues are comparing the first witness statements.

'They all agree,' says Stepanovic. 'Tobias Rösch isn't particularly popular, but he's not regarded as a total arsehole either. Nobody quite understands why it should have been him of all people lying in that cage, but nobody is especially sorry that someone from management took a thrashing. Staff morale is poor. They're cutting back the editorial departments and they're following the usual pattern: first, long-serving employees get the chop; then freelancers are forced into lousy contracts; and it ends up with someone doing two jobs for a third of the money.'

'Generally speaking,' says Sahin, 'there are two opinions among the staff. One: the management is incompetent. Or two: the management is greedy. But I get the feeling that there's more to it than that. While they're telling us a lot, they know perfectly well what they'd better not say.'

'Awkward,' I say.

'Unsatisfactory,' says Sahin, looking steadfastly at me in that way only women who know exactly who they are can pull off. 'But not exactly unusual.'

Her hands are resting on the table, on the fanned-out witness statements. She's pushed the coffee away slightly and not yet touched it. Her hair is swept strictly back behind her ears; the corners of her mouth twitch almost imperceptibly. I like her tough air.

'Bodo and Daniel are over at Mohn & Wolff, having another crack at the staff,' says Stepanovic. 'Plus, we've since learnt that Tobias Rösch lives with a girlfriend. They're expecting a baby. Rösch himself isn't up to being questioned yet – or at least that's what the doctors say.'

'Ivo and I will drive over to see the girlfriend around noon,' says Sahin.

OK. So they're on first-name terms already. I hope they don't intend to get matey with me, and I take a hasty gulp of coffee.

'Good, very good,' I say, slightly at random, and Stepanovic responds with just the look I deserve: irritation. I take another gulp. 'How many witness statements do we have now?'

'We're up to about eighty,' says Stepanovic.

'Which is a joke, given that there are two thousand employees there,' says Sahin. 'We'll have to think of something.'

'How many people are there at management level?' I ask.

'About a hundred and fifty,' she says.

'And on the works council?'

'Seventeen,' says Stepanovic.

'That's doable,' I say.

'Or else I can get a few more people on it,' says Stepanovic.

Sahin raises her eyebrows again, in that almost painful way, as if to say: that'll empty the station.

'When we've been to Rösch's girlfriend's, we can drive over there and help out,' she says. 'Four of us should be able to get through it in a couple of days. I'll call the guys now and tell them to concentrate on the management and works council. And then we'll widen the circle.'

She clears her throat.

'Although I reckon the management are the last people we'll get anything useful from.'

Stepanovic coughs a touch too loudly.

Well. If that isn't a forewarning of a power struggle, I'll eat my hat.

'By the way, what did forensics say about the cage?' I ask, before they go for each other's throats.

'It's just as Daniel thought,' says Sibel Sahin. 'A dog transporter, made in China, probably ordered online for convenience. There was no precise match for that weird, old-fashioned padlock. The guys reckon it might be a "collector's item", and that it might have come from a circus or something.'

'Any interesting evidence?' I ask.

'Nothing,' she says. 'Only Tobias Rösch's DNA. The culprit was very careful and very thorough. He or she had more than just gloves to hand.'

The word 'gloves' lodges in my head, and that's probably a sign that I should go, so I stand up, thank them, and I'm out of there.

I spend the rest of the day in my room, pondering. Calabretta would have taken me along to question the witnesses, just for fun.

That evening, I call him, because you should do that if you've thought about someone a couple of times in a day. And, hey, we go out for pizza.

VIKTOR AND CHARITY

Inspector Calabretta's favourite pizzeria isn't a traditional pizzeria, but one of those achingly hip meeting places for blokes with beards. There are a few heavy wooden benches and tables inside, and a few light wooden benches and tables outside; the pizza is cooked in an open kitchen, and the pizza chefs, who are constantly pulling faces in front of the oven, are long, thin, guys and girls. They don't all have dreads, but tattoos seem to be compulsory. Over their tats they wear black jeans and white T-shirts and everything's covered in flour. On one hand, the whole thing is wonderfully uncomplicated, but on the other, it's a bit like an anarchic Starbucks, which is irritating because you have to build your own pizza, while answering a whole heap of questions:

'Ordinary flour or gluten free?'

'Ordinary.'

'With tomato sauce or bianca?'

'Tomato sauce.'

'Mozzarella or vegan cheese?'

'Mozzarella, please.'

'OK. And what toppings would you like?'

'Capers.'

'Just capers?'

'Just capers.'

'OK, Charity, you're number seventeen. Next!'

If the pizza wasn't so amazing, I'd be dishing out slapped faces all round, but first everyone would have to explain to me exactly how they wanted them.

Calabretta pushes me aside and keeps grinning goofily at me all the time the Rasta behind the bar goes through the same little game with him. Calabretta wants spicy sausage on his pizza, as always.

'Salsiccia or chorizo?'

'Salsiccia.'

'Calabrian or Neapolitan?'

'Neapolitan.'

'Parsley, basil or oregano?'

'Oregano.'

'OK, Viktor, you're number eighteen. Next!'

We grab two bottles of beer from the fridge and go outside. I sincerely hope that Calabretta can feel my knife-sharp glare on the back of his neck – for always letting him drag me here.

'For all their song and dance about Neapolitan pizza, they don't know the name Vito?' I hiss once we're sitting outside on the wooden bench right next to the wall, our backs leaning against the warm stone. There's a dual carriageway in front of us and a crossroads to our right. Rush-hour traffic, an inner-city idyll. The air is a bit less humid than yesterday, but still warm.

'Come on, you know how good their shit is,' he says, opening the beers with my lighter. 'I'll live with being called Viktor for that, Charity.'

Woah.

Dude.

I shake my head, we clink bottles and drink beer. We haven't seen each other for a few weeks, so I'd like to ask him what's new, but that would definitely be one too many questions. In this pizza place you need a break from questions for a while. Questions can be the most annoying things.

'Now, just imagine this is all a beautiful piazza,' says Calabretta. 'No traffic, a fountain in the middle with some kind of marble kid on the top, prancing about in the nude, the window blinds are slowly starting to roll up in all the houses all around, a couple of old ladies squabbling somewhere, a few pigeons here, a few rats there. Heaven.'

'Pigeons and rats, we can do,' I say. To our left is an industrial bin, which is totally buzzing with activity. Rustling, rattling, hissing. Maybe there's a cat in there too. 'And if you want a piazza with squabbling women, head for Hans-Albers-Platz.'

He reaches for the cigarette packet lying on the table in front of me.

'May I?'

'Course.'

I light two cigarettes and hand him one.

'I'm pissed off with the Kiez right now,' he says. 'Too much work.'

'What's up?'

Dammit, I did ask. I lose.

'Oh, we've been working forever on a death in a brothel – an Eastern European woman with no papers. Everything points to suicide, but we don't believe that because it was only by coincidence that we were there before anybody could vanish her. We're inclined to think that there have been other deaths around the brothel that we don't know about. An informer told us about women in that same joint who vanish once they're worn out. And apparently, they wear out very quickly, at least if those guys have anything to do with it. Thirty clients a day, and not always any proper food.'

He drains his beer and puts the bottle down. He grew up in Altona and he can drink faster than the fastest gun in the West.

'It's a nasty, complicated story and we're not making any progress. And now we've got a hit-and-run to top it off.'

He stands up.

'D'you want another beer?'

I hold my bottle up to the light and nod. A hit-and-run. Interesting.

'Tell me about this hit-and-run,' I say, when he comes back with two full bottles.

'I'd have put money on you wanting to know more about the dead prostitutes.'

'The other night I walked past an accident that looked like it had only just happened,' I say. 'And the car that knocked the woman off her bike was gone. I can't shake it off, somehow.'

'Was that on Breite Strasse, down towards Grosse Elbstrasse?' he asks.

I nod and put my beer away.

'Yeah,' he says, 'we're dealing with that now.'

'Got anyone yet?'

Suddenly my throat feels corset-tight; I can't imagine polishing off a load of cheese-topped dough any time soon.

'Contradictory witness reports,' he says, 'but at least there are some. It was probably a dark-blue BMW, which would also fit with what forensics have found.'

'Number?'

'Not yet. But there'll be an appeal in the paper tomorrow, and it's already up on social media. Sometimes that draws an amazing amount of evidence out of the woodwork.'

He twitches his lower jaw from side to side, then stretches his neck muscles. Pretty decent neck muscles. Shoulders too. Suddenly everything looks so professional. Which wasn't the case until fairly recently. It's not that long ago that he was on the floor, a heap of lovelorn misery. Right now, he looks like the exact opposite of that edition of Calabretta. So robust. There's something almost Robert de Niro-like in this slightly greying version.

'You been doing weights lately?'

He chokes on his beer and coughs.

'It's only because of my back,' he mumbles into his stubble then keeps on coughing, clears his throat laboriously and coughs again.

'Hey, it's all right,' I say. 'Looks good.'

I thump him on the back, half to signify support and half to make him finally stop coughing.

'We've got a new colleague,' he says quietly. He almost whispers it, almost as if this were a real secret. Then he looks at me big-eyed. 'She's so young.'

'Nice,' I say. 'Youngsters on the team are always exciting.'

'I feel like an old crock,' he says, lighting another couple of cigarettes for us. You can do that now you've done such a good job of stopping coughing, I think.

'Rubbish, Calabretta. You're not an old crock.'

'You ask Schulle and Brückner. One of them's in the police gym with me, sweating over the machines, the other's in training for some kind of extreme triathlon.'

Boys. Honestly.

'Is she good, then, this newbie?' I ask, dragging on my cigarette.

Calabretta looks at me, nods meaningfully and at once his eyes are radiant. Oh God. They're all infatuated with her.

'Oh, boy,' I say.

And then there's a Rastafarian pizza chef standing reproachfully by our table with a cartwheel-sized pizza on each arm: 'Hey, Viktor, I've been stood calling your numbers for hours, man.'

SHADOWRUNNER

Here's the hot iron, the saw, the squared timber.
  Here are the rusty pliers and all the bits of old dental kit.
  The blocks of wood, the willow rods, the belts.
  So, now, here's the question: with or without chloroform?

IT GENERALLY RAINS CRUD

Stepanovic has clearly delegated the job of organising chauffeur services to Inspector Ippig.

'Mr Stepanovic is on his way and he'll pick you up in ten minutes. He'd like you to be there.'

'Be where?'

It's just after eight; I've only just woken up; my eyes are as narrow as the gaps between the clouds in the sky.

'We've got a second cage.'

It's like someone's given me a shot of adrenaline.

I hang up, hastily swallow a gulp of coffee, leap into the shower and notice that I'm surprisingly unsurprised that another man's been locked in another cage. The sense that it was only a matter of time. Then the sense that time is suddenly running fast. That there are booster rockets firing in my veins. Nine minutes later, I'm standing outside the front door.

Stepanovic turns the corner in his brown Mercedes. Tyres squealing again. Either he's seen *French Connection* a few too many times, or the car badly needs work.

'Nice,' he says, as I get in.

'Do you mean me or the second cage?'

He gives me a sideways glance that's a fraction too long. I grab the seatbelt and slide down a bit in the seat. At once it feels exactly the way it always feels to sit in an old Merc: if I didn't know better, I'd think we were going on holiday.

'Do we know who it is yet?' I ask.

He shakes his head.

'The guys at the station only got the call fifteen minutes ago.'

Outside it's art nouveau in pastel shades, all nicely done up in the last few years. But you can't get rid of the grey aura – it's as if the rain on St Pauli is crud rather than water.

I stretch, can't help another yawn. Hello. Wake up, woman in my head. And you lot behind the windows, you wake up too. It's mad how bleary this part of town is in the mornings. You can't work like that though. I try to get a handle on things:

'At least it looks like someone reacted straight away this time.'

'That's true. Things went faster this time. They left Rösch lying around for quite a while.'

Stepanovic turns onto the fastest road out of St Pauli.

'Until absolutely everyone had had a chance to see him.'

'Maybe a few people are starting to shit themselves,' I say.

'Maybe,' he says. 'After all, they might well wake up in a cage themselves one morning.'

I wonder how many cages whoever it was must've bought on the internet and ask: 'What did Tobias Rösch's girlfriend say? Any enemies? You saw her yesterday, didn't you?'

'Yes, we did. She's a funny woman.'

He cuts up a taxi driver and beeps at him.

'Haven't you got a siren with you?' I ask, pointing upwards. I'd love to see his face when he slaps that most macho of warning signals onto the roof.

'Yeah,' he says. 'But it makes me look silly. I'd rather drive without one if I don't have to.'

Well, look at that. But you still scared that taxi driver.

'What do you mean, "funny woman"?' I ask.

'Well, kind of plasticky,' he says. 'Like a fabulous Barbie. Seriously pregnant but immaculately styled. Opened the door in high heels and a tight dress, and her blonde hair looked like she'd just come from a salon. Anyway, I found her funny.'

Give way to the right? Sod that.

'And I didn't get the impression she was worried or anything. I mean, her bloke was kidnapped and assaulted and shoved in a cage. Aren't pregnant women meant to react differently? And she only noticed that he hadn't been there overnight when we rang her.'

'As far as I know, pregnant women have the same range of reactions as anyone else, depending on what kind of person they are.'

'OK,' he waggles his head and pulls a sad face. 'Thanks, Sherlock.'

'You're welcome, Watson.' I wind down the window and lean my head to the right. Ah, the wind in my hair. 'She might just be a stupid cow.'

'In any case, she wasn't going to pull out a winning lottery ball for us,' says Stepanovic. 'In her opinion, Tobias Rösch has no enemies of any kind, and even if she isn't really all that interested in him, he'll be the perfect father for her child. Direct quote, or at least the second part is.'

He pokes two cigarettes out of his trouser pocket. He lights one and holds the other out to me.

'No, thanks,' I say. 'It's still too early.'

He looks at me like I'm not quite all there.

'Give me half an hour, OK?'

'OK,' he says, utterly baffled.

Despite the open window, it's as hot in the car as if it were mid-August at midday.

NOBODY'LL BE ALONG TO PICK UP THE SMILE

The man doesn't look good at all. His ribcage is rising and falling at about a hundred times the normal rate, his left hand is shaking, large expanses of his body are covered with everything that hurts: cuts, scrapes, burns, bruises. And he's awake. Lying unconscious in cages seems to have gone out of fashion. His eyes stare fixedly at Officer Lienen, who's at work with an even bigger bolt-cutter than last time while talking quietly to the man. Kneeling right next to Lienen is a paramedic, probably saying the same stuff. You know, all the things you tell people in dreadful situations: keep calm, we'll get you out of there, it's going to be OK. Although obviously nothing's going to be OK for a while yet.

I'm glad to see that Sahin seems to have brought Lienen along, regardless. He's got one of these outsized, old-fashioned padlocks off before, so he can do it a second time. The lock looks pretty much exactly like the first one, maybe a bit rustier and the corners aren't as rounded, but the calibre's the same.

Lienen groans once or twice, then there's a crack and a crunch and the thing's broken. He holds the cage door open, and the paramedic crawls towards the man – a somewhat pasty blond – and lays that old favourite, the foil blanket, around his shoulders. Lienen stands up, takes off his uniform cap and wipes the sweat from his brow.

I try to throw a smile his way, but it doesn't quite make it. It crashes against the glass façade behind the cage and slips to the floor with an unpleasant squeal. I don't think anyone'll be along to pick it up today.

'Ippig and Acolatse are talking to the receptionist,' says Sahin with a minimal nod in the direction of the building. She looks at me with a grim steadfastness, perhaps with a deep awareness that all this is perfectly normal.

I try to make out what's going on in the foyer. Lo and behold, it's practically nothing. My two colleagues are standing at the curved reception desk talking to the pastel-coloured young woman that Stepanovic and I spoke to a couple of days ago. Otherwise, the place looks deserted. As if everyone has taken cover in their offices. But at the same time, it's as though I can see a thousand eyes behind the mirrored-glass façade, watching us and the naked man in his foil.

Acolatse is the first to come through the revolving door. He's holding a pad and a pen.

'Leonhard Bohnsen,' he says. 'Apparently the publishing director for the magazines division.'

'Yes,' a quiet voice emerges from the foil, 'yes, that's me.'

We're all standing around the cage in no time. His hand has stopped shaking and his breathing seems to have returned to normal too. Tough guy, this Bohnsen.

'Who did this?' asks Stepanovic. All of us know what he means by 'this'.

'A shadow,' he says, and with that his hand starts trembling again. 'A big, black shadow.'

He tries to sit up – he doesn't want to lie in the cage any longer, which I find entirely understandable, but it would be undignified to pull him out of there. The paramedic is doing his best to soften the situation. Fiddling with the golden foil, for example.

Some things are just futile.

'A shadow?' asks Stepanovic, dropping to his knees and holding on to the bars.

A second paramedic arrives; he's got a stretcher under his arm and he's firing out fierce glares.

'Come on, leave the man in peace for the moment,' he says. He's obviously the member of the rescue party who sets the tone; that's something you always spot right away. 'You can ask questions later, at the hospital.'

Then the two paramedics manage, somewhat clumsily, to pull Leonhard Bohnsen out of the cage and heave him onto the stretcher, although you just have to look at his face to see that he doesn't want to be put on it. Then they take him away. Stepanovic looks like someone's snatched his toy from him.

'It'll be fine,' says Sahin, patting him on the shoulder.

In the meantime, Ippig's emerged too. He watches the victim and the paramedics as they leave, pulls on a pair of gloves and says: 'Shall we?'

At the prospect of taking the crime scene apart properly and so promptly, a vicious little smile flits across Stepanovic's face.

MEN IN CAGES ARE UNDERSTANDABLE

'Bloody takeaway-coffee culture,' says Stepanovic. 'The whole place is heaving with paper cups.'

He's spent the morning in Mohn & Wolff's editorial departments while I was in my office destroying a few files; now we're sitting in his car again, on the way to the hospital to speak to Leonhard Bohnsen and hopefully also to Tobias Rösch. Sahin, Ippig and Acolatse are still questioning the staff.

'And?' I ask. 'You must have found out about more than just their overpriced coffee habit.'

'I hate to admit it, but that's about all we've learnt. They're all acting like they have no idea what might have led to the two attacks. It's as though they've agreed among themselves to kindly hold their tongues.'

'Have they?'

He shrugs.

'Dunno, but if they have, we've got our work cut out. Journalists are used to keeping secrets. The others are ploughing on with the interviews, but I don't think we'll get any important information that way. And, who knows, maybe it really hasn't got anything to do with their colleagues? Maybe we're barking up completely the wrong tree.'

'It's the only tree we've got right now.'

'Hm.'

'And it makes sense to me,' I say. 'I mean, it's all understandable.'

'You think caged managers are understandable?'

'Don't you?'

'No. However many skeletons somebody has in the closet, he doesn't belong in a cage. We're not living in the Middle Ages.'

'I wouldn't do it myself,' I say, 'but I can see why someone might.'

He lights a cigarette for himself and holds out the box towards me.

'Thanks, I've got one,' I say and light one of my own.

'Sahin and I went to see Grabowski again today,' he says. 'I mean, it's sick what they're doing to their people there. Perhaps you're right and they're all steadily losing their grip.'

In my opinion, the whole idea that one person's the boss and can tell other people what to do is fundamentally sick, but nobody asks me.

'Here's an example of a new idea from management,' says Stepanovic. 'It's been around for a couple of weeks and was allegedly floated by Leonhard Bohnsen. Every Monday, staff are supposed to give their line managers suggestions for how to reduce costs. So, freelancers tell the editors, editors tell their heads of department, and heads of department tell their editors-in-chief, who are meant to implement the ideas. The official line is that this ought to help streamline processes, because it's only when you really know the processes that you can see what wastes too much time, and therefore too much money.'

He drags on his cigarette and takes the corner with squealing tyres.

'In practice of course,' he says, 'all it produces is stressed staff.'

He stops at a red light and looks at me.

'Because either you come up with a way to rationalise your colleague, or, if you're unlucky, your colleague has a great idea that means eventually you're the one being rationalised.'

The light goes green, he accelerates, the tyres scream.

'It's a dirty trick, if you ask me.'

Men who give lectures.

'Pretty dirty trick,' I say.

Yet nobody's supposed to feel like torturing the people responsible for a trick like that.

I drag on my cigarette again and chuck it out of the window. Tastes foul.

'Oh, by the way,' I say, 'Tobias Rösch is apparently fit enough to answer questions now. I rang the hospital earlier. And this morning, Bohnsen was positively dying to talk to us, wasn't he?'

'Sorry, did you take that seriously?' Stepanovic rolls his eyes. 'He was talking about a shadow. Watch out or he'll start telling us about the Demon King.'

'OK, so that bit sounded slightly nuts,' I say, staring out of the window.

But every shadow has to be cast by something. He must have seen something.

'The doctor said on the phone that both of them had injuries caused most likely by rusty tools and red-hot objects.'

Stepanovic is driving decidedly too slowly by his standards; he fiddles around with the radio and grimaces.

'I always did find tools nasty.'

FLASHY-THINGED

Tobias Rösch is lying on his side, looking out of the window. He still looks seriously ropey. But I get the impression his misery has been drizzled with a teaspoon of self-pity, which keeps my sympathy in check, because I can't stand self-pity. My dad, the former army officer, had his own attitude towards it: bravery helps. I find that bravery doesn't help against everything, but the phrase is always clear in the back of my mind. Just in case, and certainly in cases of self-pity.

Rösch has pulled his hospital blanket right up to his ears, even though it's sweltering in his room. The nurse who brought us to him starts by opening the window.

'The fresh air will do you good, Mr Rösch,' she says and, without waiting for a reaction, flits out of the room again with a coquettish smile.

Stepanovic is not unimpressed by her nurse-like performance; he stands somewhat awkwardly in the middle of the room for a while, taking a moment to get himself together.

He clears his throat, I position myself at the foot of the bed and try to speak to Tobias Rösch.

'Mr Rösch?'

'You're not the nurse.'

A trembling voice under the blankets.

'True. My name is Riley, I'm the public prosecutor for your case. And I've brought my colleague, Stepanovic from the Serious Crime Office.'

'We'd like to ask you a few questions,' says Stepanovic.

Aha. My colleague's back to normal.

Tobias Rösch turns to face us and pushes the blanket down a little.

OK, I was seriously wrong about the self-pity thing. The man truly seems deeply disturbed. He looks like a startled animal; his eyes dart from side to side at incredible speed, from me to Stepanovic and back again, on a continuous loop. And then there are all the cuts and scrapes on his face. I feel sorry for him.

'Don't worry,' I say. 'We won't hurt you.'

Stepanovic grabs a couple of chairs and pulls them over to the bed; we sit down.

'How are you doing?' I ask.

'Fine,' says Rösch, 'fine. I've got everything here and it's such lovely weather…'

His eyes wander briefly out of the window and then back to me, to Stepanovic, to me, to Stepanovic – just watching him is enough to send you completely crazy.

And the weather isn't the least bit lovely. It's humid and the sky is hung with cloud. Rösch is clearly talking nonsense.

'The psychologist,' Stepanovic whispers in my direction. 'We need the psychologist.'

'And maybe a few tranquilisers,' I whisper back.

Rösch's attention flitters up to the ceiling and to the door, then it's back to us, in some form or other.

'Great,' he says. 'I'm doing great.'

What follows is probably meant to be a smile. But it derails and turns into a grotesque rictus that puts me in mind of various high-ranking Marvel baddies.

'Can you tell us what happened to you?' I ask.

'A shadow,' he says. 'There was a shadow.'

Stepanovic looks at me, I look at Stepanovic, and I reckon he's thinking the same as me: no way?

'What did the shadow do?' he asks.

'Nothing. But I was scared. Very scared. Only scared. And then I woke up in a cage.'

His eyes dart to our faces.

'You were there too.'

'That's right,' I say. 'We were there when you woke up.'

'And the police. And then an ambulance came.'

'That's right,' says Stepanovic. He looks at me and raises his right eyebrow.

We're talking to a child. It's hard to imagine this man as head of HR. Somebody must have flashy-thinged his mind.

Stepanovic stands up, takes his chair and pulls it round to the side of the bed, so that he can sit as close to Tobias Rösch as possible.

'What can you remember?'

'When I saw the shadow for the first time, it wasn't that big. But later, when I woke up the first time and saw the shadow again, it was really big. Twice as tall as me.'

'When you woke up the first time?'

'Yes. I was in this room.'

'What kind of room?'

Rösch shrugs, eight times maybe. His sleek, dark hair falls onto his face.

'I couldn't move. I couldn't see much either. Just the shadow. And the fact that he had something big in his hand. Then I got scared. And then I was in the cage.'

He turns his head away from Stepanovic and looks at me. For the first time since we arrived, he manages to hold his gaze steady.

'I was in a cage, wasn't I?'

I nod cautiously. I don't want to draw his attention too much onto me; I want him to stay with Stepanovic.

'Where did you see the shadow the first time?' he asks.

'In the car park,' says Rösch.

'Which car park?'

'The car park under the office.'

'The basement car park?'

'Yes.'

Wow. This is tough.

Stepanovic remains relaxed. He looks long and calmly at Rösch before asking his next question.

'What do you think of Leonhard Bohnsen?'

Tobias Rösch looks at my colleague as if he's just bitten off a budgerigar's head. Then his face lights up, but it's a will-o'-the-wisp kind of brightness, as if there were something very dark lurking beneath it.

'Leo,' he says with a cackle. And repeats: 'Leo!'

He turns back to me; he seems concerned to share this with the woman in the room: 'We went to school together.'

DEMENTORS
(THE BIRDS DIED IN TINY CRATES)

'That's right, we were at the same boarding school.'

Leonhard Bohnsen is sitting up in bed, typing on his smartphone. Stepanovic is standing by the window, arms crossed. I'm leaning against the wall, kind of nearby, making an effort not to stick my hands in my trouser pockets. Not really a great look.

Mind you, Bohnsen doesn't seem remotely bothered what we do or how we act. He's probably one of those guys who's only interested in himself. And he's not particularly fazed by being plastered and stapled from top to toe, being painted with antibacterial salve or by being draped, however scantily, in a hospital gown.

'That's looking inflamed,' says Stepanovic, pointing at a red, swollen patch under the butterfly stitch above Bohnsen's right collarbone.

'Oh.'

Bohnsen looks up from his phone for a few seconds and presses the buzzer beside his bed.

'What school were you at, then?' I ask.

My father used to wonder if it mightn't be sensible to look for a boarding-school place for me. You know, cos my mum was gone, and he was alone with me, and his work for the US Army ... Looking back, I understand that it sometimes seemed too much for him. But at the time, I found the idea totally out of order. It sucked enough not having a mum – I didn't want to be without a dad too. And I thought we managed pretty well. So, to this day, the words 'boarding school' kick back at me like a mule. When I hear 'boarding school', the back of my neck cracks, and suddenly images of loneliness blow up in my face.

My dad and me, eating at the table, hands next to our plates and, above the table, a silence pressing down on our heads.

My dad and me at night, each in our own room and our own bed, just a few metres apart yet an ocean between us, because someone was sobbing in their sleep.

My dad and me at Christmas, sitting round the tree, as if we've been set there as decorations, but really lousy ones.

Of course, it wasn't always like that – we had noisy and cosy and fun times together too. My dad had a dry, wicked sense of humour that I liked a lot; and he had a big heart too – couldn't bear to see anyone suffer. He kept bringing starving cats and sick birds home. The cats left us when they were no longer hungry, the birds died in tiny crates, and with every lost cat and every dead bird, a little more of my dad's soul was chafed away, leaving it raw. And then there was that moment when Christopher Riley was completely overwhelmed. Well, nobody had told him in advance, let alone taught him, what life would be like: a single-parent-soldier in a foreign country that, right up to his death, saw him only as an occupier and never as a guest. He'd thought he'd come as a liberator. And then life liberated him, bit by bit, of happiness.

I can't remember ever having seen a gleam in my dad's eyes.

'At Biesendorf,' says Bohnsen, typing. This bloke's so rude, in comparison my manners look like Swedish court etiquette. 'Little village down south.'

The door opens, the nurse comes in – *the* nurse, the one who was in Tobias Rösch's room earlier. Stepanovic gets all wide-eyed again, and now I know why he said that about the sore spot, which doesn't look any more inflamed to my eyes than any of the other wounds on Leonhard Bohnsen's body.

The nurse looks at the place, says 'mm' and 'aha'; Stepanovic looks at the nurse, goes 'hmm' and exhales through his lips. I look at Stepanovic, standing there, tall as a tree, his lugubrious, pleasantly furrowed face framed by thick black-grey hair, his broad shoulders packaged in his dark-blue shirt, his legs in threadbare jeans, his feet in black ankle boots, his hands at that moment discarded God knows where on his own body, and I think: astute and slick and lost all at once.

The nurse dabs a neat blob of iodine ointment on the possibly extremely inflamed sore, and says that maybe, all things considered, Bohnsen needs some antibiotics after all.

Once she's gone again, everyone hastily catches their breath. And in mid-breath, Stepanovic says, as quickly as if he'd inhaled a fireman: 'Why should you two in particular be the victims of this cage business?'

Bohnsen looks up from his phone and pulls an outraged face.

'You'd have to ask certain people in the editorial departments at Mohn & Wolff about that. There's a certain clique who consider management to be practically the devil's own army. They just won't see that, without the work we do, their jobs would have vanished long ago.'

'But you don't get put in a cage and tortured for that,' I say.

He actually manages to look down on me, even though he's in bed and I'm standing up.

'There are people at the company who truly hate me. You could start by considering them.'

'In the last year, you've taken the decision to lay off loads of people,' I say, 'so it's hardly surprising that some staff might find it difficult to enjoy their work.'

Bohnsen narrows his eyes to slits and crimps his lips. He has pink skin, he's blond, he's pasty: he looks like a cartoon piglet.

'A dyed-in-the-wool leftie, eh, Madam Prosecutor?'

'Officer's daughter with anarchic leanings. How about you?'

All of a sudden, I feel that I want to hurt him.

He doesn't answer.

'When we found Tobias Rösch the day before yesterday,' Stepanovic says, 'we thought at first that it must be something to do with the situation in the company. But now we know that you two were at school together and have obviously been victims of the same person, the position has clearly changed somewhat.'

'Hm,' says Bohnsen and starts typing on his phone again. He seems to be thinking. He seems to need the phone to think. To exist. Perhaps, if he put it aside, there'd be a pop, and he'd be gone.

Stepanovic steps over to the bed and, without asking, sits down on the edge, getting right up close to Bohnsen. If it were me in the bed, I'd find it uncomfortable, even if he weren't so close.

'You said you were attacked by a shadow. Tobias Rösch says the same. What should we be taking from all this?'

Bohnsen lays his smartphone on the white bedside table and scoots a little over towards the other side of the bed. Astonishingly, there's no pop – Stepanovic is crowding him so much that Bohnsen doesn't even have room to disappear.

'Well, obviously it wasn't a real shadow. But the disguise was good. I wore something like it at Halloween once. You can get them anywhere online. What are they called? Those *Harry Potter* things that keep trying to suck people's souls out. Oh hell…'

He reaches for his phone and starts typing again.

'Dementors,' says Stepanovic, as if knowing that stuff was nothing special.

The serious crime experts read kids' books?

And so do publishing executives?

'They're the guys!' says Bohnsen, putting his head to one side and pointing at Stepanovic. He's properly thrilled. 'That's what the chap looked like. But for real. Must be something to do with the stuff he drugged me with. Wasn't bad, I must say.'

'Drugs?' I ask.

'Beats me what it was, but he must have pumped me full of something. I was in the car park, on the way to my car, and suddenly someone grabs me from behind and holds a rag to my face. And when I come round, I'm lying in a room, tied up, and there's this shadow standing in front of me.'

'What did he use to cause all these injuries?' asks Stepanovic.

'I don't know. He didn't touch me while I was awake. He just looked at me through a kind of black veil that he had over his face. And then I had another rag on my nose, and when I woke up in that cage, it was like this,' he points to his upper body, his cheeks, his forehead. 'And, well, you saw the rest.'

'Do you have any idea who could be angry enough with you and Tobias Rösch that they'd do such a thing?' I ask.

Bohnsen clutches his smartphone to his bruised chest. Then he looks at Stepanovic, his fellow *Harry Potter* fan and co-nurse-admirer. He looks at him openly and honestly, as if a curious trust has developed between the two of them in just a few minutes.

'Perhaps you ought to talk to Sebastian. Don't want him to land up in a bloody box too.'

'Who is Sebastian?' asks Stepanovic.

'Sebastian Schmidt, our chief executive,' says Bohnsen. 'Sebastian was at school with Tobias and me. We were roommates.'

'The *three* of you were at boarding school?' I ask. 'And now the three of you are on the board of Mohn & Wolff?'

Bohnsen doesn't understand the question.

And my colleague Stepanovic looks at me and says: 'That's normal, isn't it?'

Sure. Totally normal. I get my apparently mixed-up brain gyrations in gear and ask: 'Is there anyone else we ought to speak to? Do you and Tobias Rösch and Sebastian have other friends from that time? Or anyone close to you now?'

Bohnsen looks past Stepanovic, out of the window. He seems to think properly for the first time since we've been here. As if he would never have come up with such an insane question in all his life. Then he turns his head to me and answers robotically: 'No.'

VERY BAD SECRETARY

Sebastian Schmidt is unavailable, says the receptionist.

We decline to believe her and fight our way through to his secretary.

'He's unavailable,' she says.

'It's important,' I say, playing the public prosecutor card.

Luxuriant view over the harbour, even from the anteroom. All the way to the *MS Cap San Diego*. Not bad. But unfortunately, a very bad secretary. I give her my normal scornful glare, and in less than thirty seconds, she's given her boss away. Three sips of coffee, two glances out of the window – I follow her gaze – and, hey presto, she says: 'Dr Schmidt is currently with his solicitor, Dr Beiersdorfer at the police headquarters. As far as I know, he's giving a witness statement.'

At the police HQ?

With his solicitor?

For a witness statement?

'What kind of witness statement?' I ask.

She shrugs her shoulders and sips her coffee again.

We're on the road faster than the girl can whip out her nail file.

TWO WANNABES FOR THE EUROPEAN PARLIAMENT

Stepanovic drives us to the northern suburbs in his usual racy style, and I make the calls that will tell us exactly where Sebastian Schmidt is right now. He's with the murder squad, sitting in the office of Detective Chief Inspector Vito Calabretta. Schmidt is sitting with Calabretta to discuss a fatal hit-and-run.

But he's not sitting there as a witness.

He's sitting there as the chief suspect.

'Well, there's a thing,' I say.

'What?' asks Stepanovic.

'Strange coincidence.'

'Coincidences are always strange,' he says, 'but they make life a beautiful dance, don't you think?'

He gives me a rather smarmy Jean-Paul Belmondo look and whistles a little tune that I don't know, or don't recognise.

Until five seconds ago, I'd have sworn blind that Stepanovic was a second-generation immigrant from Offenbach or Höchst, or another of Frankfurt's more colourful suburbs, but after the sentence he's just uttered, I wouldn't lay a cent on it now. I wonder whether he actually comes from Montmartre and spends his evenings secretly singing French chansons. As we drive up to the HQ, he gives the tyres the regulation spin.

At the barrier, he languidly holds his pass up to the windscreen, and the task of saying a polite hello falls to me. My new partner constantly veers between a charm offensive and just plain offensive. This is increasingly pushing me into the role of the nice, down-to-earth woman from the Prosecution Service, and I'm not sure how long I can sustain it. At this moment, face to face with the porter in his porter's lodge, it feels like an overly tight roll-neck jumper.

The porter raises the barrier and waves us through.

Stepanovic parks the car in the first visitor's space we find. Ten minutes later, we're standing in the hot spot – the murder squad office.

Big hello with Schulle and Brückner.

'Hey, Ms Riley, long time no see!'

'What are you doing here?'

I introduce them both to Stepanovic and tell them what we're doing here – namely, looking for Sebastian Schmidt.

'No way? That's insane,' says Schulle. 'The boss is in there with your man, along with a lawyer and our new colleague.'

The new colleague. She seems to be a topic of conversation between Schulle and Brückner too, because at the word 'colleague', a silly grin flits from one of their faces to the other. I bet she's got red hair.

'How long have they been in there?' I ask.

'A good hour,' says Brückner. 'It's cut and dried, more or less. This morning we got two independent witness statements that agreed on Schmidt's number plate, and a third witness gave a relatively good description of the man behind the wheel. He's basically not getting out of here. His BMW is down in forensics too. Admittedly it's just been through the car wash, but they're bound to find something.'

'He hasn't confessed yet?' I ask.

'We'd have heard if he had,' says Schulle.

'I happened to pass the accident on Saturday night,' I say.

Stepanovic is standing slightly behind me, which I find strangely comforting and discomforting at the same time.

'It was grim. I'm glad you've pulled someone in so quickly.'

'Meet the professionals,' says Brückner with the grin that he always grins when he launches a little showboat. 'And what do you two want with our chief suspect?'

'We'd like to talk to him about his schooldays,' says Stepanovic.

'And we have to consider putting him under protection. It's possible that someone wants to get at him.'

Schulle and Brückner look like they're about to bark at us. I realise that they don't think much of getting protection for a man who's just run a young woman over in his fancy car and then run away. I don't think much of it either. But I don't think we'll be able to avoid it.

'Can we wait here until DCI Calabretta's finished with him?' asks Stepanovic.

'You can,' says Brückner, heading off in search of coffee for everyone. I watch him go. After the long summer, he really is outrageously blond and freckled. And Schulle looks the same. Some Hamburg boys must be delivered that way. It shouldn't be allowed, except on farms and in surfing regions.

When Calabretta's office door opens, I hear someone say that, after all, there's no risk of absconding, to which a woman's voice answers that, in a case of hit-and-run, she wouldn't necessarily share that view.

Through the door comes a tall, broad-shouldered guy in a grey suit. He has bushy red-brown hair, horn-rims, a beard, and holds a briefcase under his arm. Behind him appears a less tall but equally broad-shouldered man in a brown cord suit with black hipster glasses. His dark-blond hair has a severe parting; his designer stubble is clipped and impeccably styled. There's something uncommonly boyish about him, but he's trying to hide it beneath the glasses, hair and beard. Behind the two men, I see Calabretta and a dainty woman with masses of tight strawberry-blonde curls, which were probably tied back in a bun this morning. She has a pretty, slightly wry face and a disrespectful expression; her slim body is clad in a faded, dark-grey sweatshirt and jeans. She looks like a small, dangerous girl.

Calabretta forgets that he ought to be puzzled by seeing me and smiles broadly; then he checks himself and says: 'Well, there's a thing.'

Before anyone who presents no risk of absconding can scarper, I explain who everybody is and introduce the mysterious Mr

Stepanovic once again. Calabretta nods and looks at his colleague from SCO 44 in a way I know and dislike: it's a junk-measuring way, which, obviously, I dislike because I've got the biggest balls of anyone here.

The red-haired girl doesn't wait for the boys and me to finish comparing our balls – she introduces herself.

'Anne Stanislawski, hello,' she says. Her voice sounds as though she smokes a lot. Or as if she cried a lot as a child. There's a grater in her throat. Her handshake is firm and soft at the same time. Now I know why Calabretta thinks she's great: she is great. I've seldom met such a small person who fills a room so full.

Sebastian Schmidt, on the other hand, is the kind of bloke who finds that very hard to bear. Although he's positioned in a rather unfavourable light, he can hardly wait to make himself known. He looks so impatient that I expect to see his slick-arse hair start quivering any moment. Perhaps as a chief exec, he's just not used to having to wait two minutes. But here, everyone's body tension is making it absolutely plain to him that he'll have to wait. Unpleasant. Understandably.

I turn to him and deliver him from his agony.

'Mr Schmidt?'

'Yes, Sebastian Schmidt, good morning. My solicitor, Dr Beiersdorfer.' He waves his right hand at the tall, besuited chap beside him. 'And who are you, may I ask? We were about to leave.'

'Riley, Public Prosecution Service. And this is Detective Chief Inspector Stepanovic.'

'How can we help you, Ms Riley?'

It's the lawyer. He ruffles his chest feathers up a bit, trying to make himself even bigger than he already is, and straightens his horn-rims like a wannabe politician.

'I think we've answered all the questions put to us by these ladies and gentlemen – and to their satisfaction.'

Anne Stanislawski can't stop herself delivering a dry little cough into her hand.

'As for when we're satisfied,' says Calabretta, 'that's for us to decide.' That old sheriff.

'We're not concerned with your hit-and-run,' says Stepanovic.

The lawyer narrows his eyes to slits. He obviously doesn't like it when anyone says 'hit-and-run'.

'As you must have heard, this morning your publishing director, Leonhard Bohnsen, was found lying in a cage outside the company offices,' says Stepanovic to Schmidt, without honouring the solicitor with even the tiniest of glances. 'And two days ago, your head of HR, Tobias Rösch, was found in the same place.'

Sebastian Schmidt's feet begin to tap out a quiet, uneasy beat.

'Since then, we've been able to talk to them both. Leonhard Bohnsen says the three of you were at school together.'

'Yes, we were,' says Schmidt, trying to bring his feet under control. 'And?'

'We're wondering what links the attacks on the two men. Their work at Mohn & Wolff? Or your schooldays?'

'My client has very different priorities just now…'

'Leave it, Fred,' says Schmidt, raising his right hand. He looks at Stepanovic and me as if we're both children. As if he's thinking about something that has to do with picking out a team, or something like that.

'Is there somewhere quiet here where we can talk?'

'My office,' says Stepanovic.

'You can use my office again,' says Calabretta to me, pointing with his thumb at the door behind him.

I can see by Sebastian Schmidt's thin nose that he doesn't particularly want to spend another hour in the office where he's just had a professional grilling.

'Ah,' I say, 'I think the air's a bit stale in there.'

'Let's go to mine,' says Stepanovic.

Go to mine. Right you are.

YOUR OWN IMPORTANCE

'You know, there's been a lot going on in the last few days. I don't even know where to start. First of all, I'm obviously very worried about Tobi; just between ourselves, Tobi isn't a particularly strong character. And then suddenly, two days later, Leo cops it too, and so obviously I'm wondering: what is all this? Who's got it in for these two, and what does he want? And what if he wants something from me too? And why? And in the middle of all these worries, suddenly your murder-squad colleagues burst in and tell me I've knocked down and killed a young woman! You know, I didn't even drive anywhere that night. My wife can confirm that. We were sitting by the fire with a nice glass of red. My wife likes dark chocolate with hers – it's sort of our ritual. Oh, wait, sorry, that doesn't interest you, does it? There, you see, I'm getting a bit confused. I don't know what your colleagues want from me. Sure, they want to do an identification parade for these witnesses who claim to have seen me behind the wheel. But it's not quite as simple as all that, as you know. Anyway. Yes. So. We'll see. And what was it you wanted to know again, about my schooldays? You know, we were boys. At a boarding school. Well, you must know what it's like: good days and bad days, sometimes fun, sometimes not so much fun. Nothing out of the ordinary. Put it this way: I can't think of anything that could help you out over the thing with Leo and Tobi. But of course, I can't help wondering. Do I get police protection or what?'

'The three of you,' Stepanovic says, 'actually shared a room at school?'

He nods. Sebastian Schmidt nods the nod he probably always uses when he wants to look good and big and powerful – when he's just done a snazzy deal, for instance. It's a deliberate nod, his upper body touching the edge of the table, his arms folded on the tabletop, his lips very consciously laid one on top of the other. The whole movement kind of suggests the sort of 'uh-huh' that you say to someone you haven't really been listening to because what the other person has to say just doesn't matter a damn – at least not in comparison with your own importance.

'But rooms in boarding schools like that,' says Stepanovic, 'in my experience they're usually for either two or four people, aren't they?'

Sebastian Schmidt sits up a little too briskly, straightens his glasses and strokes back his hair like a gigolo.

Stepanovic looks at him and shakes his head.

'Too bad. Now you've mucked up your parting.'

FORGOTTEN

'You know,' says Sebastian Schmidt, 'we didn't have much to do with him – somehow he didn't quite measure up – I'm sure you know what I mean. He was a strange kid, often in trouble. Good grief. I'd quite forgotten him. That's nuts.'

'Wow,' says Leonhard Bohnsen. 'Nope, I can't remember his name for the life of me.'

'No,' says Tobias Rösch, 'no, no, no. Nobody. No one, no one, no one.'

Then bursts out laughing. And he doesn't stop. We can still hear him laughing as we get into the lift at the end of the hospital corridor.

OH, YOU KNOW

'Right,' says Stepanovic, 'what now? Does he get police protection?'

'My heart says no, my head says yes,' I reply. Or have I got that the wrong way round? 'But if we don't give him protection and he winds up in a cage the day after tomorrow, it'll all blow up in our faces.'

'OK,' he says. 'I'll sort it.'

We lean against his car and smoke cigarettes. It's still warm; it feels as though the clouds are wrapped around my shoulders like a blanket. I find myself thinking about my leather jacket, hanging on a chair at home. I haven't touched it since Klatsche brought it back. And not just because of the weather. There's something wrong with the jacket. There's something wrong in general.

'It's Friday evening,' I say. 'Shall we go for a drink?'

He looks at me, drags on his cigarette again and chucks it away.

'Not sure,' he says.

'About what?'

'Oh, you know.'

I don't know a thing.

At that moment, the blanket of cloud breaks open directly above us, in that unexpected and beautiful and ephemeral way that only happens in Hamburg. A ray of sunlight edges across the sky, and for a brief moment it looks as though the good Lord wants to tell us something.

I'm not sure whether it comes of defiance or carelessness, but, annoyingly, I smoke the filter too.

I look Stepanovic in the eye a little longer than is strictly necessary and say: 'I don't know what you mean.'

Then I hail a taxi and we drive to St Pauli.

HOLD ON

For the hundredth time, Klatsche has found some knackered, fly-tipped living-room furniture and arranged it on the pavement outside the Blue Night. A sofa, three armchairs and something wooden that's currently burning in an old oil drum; maybe it used to be a table or a chair – all I can make out is that it had four legs. Next to the drum is a large grill. Next to the grill is Rocco, who likes to claim that Argentinian blood, and thus the ability to barbecue meat, runs in his veins. The fact that his so-called Argentinian blood is more likely to come from the Balkans is irrelevant to this matter, and in general too. If he feels like an Argentinian, then he probably is one. He's got a poker in his hand.

In the background, towering above the houses – which are no more than three storeys high and have clubs in the cellars, bars on the ground floors, and rooms on the first and second floors that are used either to sell sex or to monitor the associated negotiations on the street – are a few harbour cranes, which look no less rusty than the rest of the composition, Rocco's barbecue included. At that moment, even the sky above all this maritime industry puts on its orange-red evening hue. And as the twilight makes St Pauli glow along with the sky, lights slowly start coming on all over the place.

'What are you up to? Planning to barbecue a whole sheep?'

'Watch out, Madam Prosecutor, I've got hold of some fantastic South American steaks for us. Hopefully Carla's at the bar, marinating the things.'

Rocco wipes the back of his hand across his forehead, leaving a black streak. As always, he's wearing slightly shabby pin-striped trousers and a shirt that shows off too much chest, although that might be at least partly because the top four buttons are missing. His brown, fuzzy curls look for all the world as if he's done a couple of barbecues already today.

'Where's Klatsche?' I ask.

'In the cellar, lugging beer crates about.'

'You look thirsty,' I say. 'I'll get us something to drink.'

'Will you marry me?'

'You're married already, Rocco.'

'My wife doesn't fancy me any more.'

'Rubbish.'

'Ask her!'

For a moment I get the feeling he might actually mean it, but something within me shoos the thought around the nearest corner.

There's music playing in the Blue Night. If I'm not mistaken, it's Billie Holliday; her sad cries scratch at my skin, wanting to reach deeper inside.

Carla's standing behind the bar; in front of her, there's a big dish; on the dish are impressive-looking steaks. She's messing about with olive oil, chilli flakes and rosemary – I think. She's wearing a white T-shirt that's a bit too tight and a black pencil skirt. She's knotted her dark curls on top of her head, but they won't stay put – another strand comes loose with every second movement and dangles round her face like a slack telephone cable. There are a few horizontal creases across her brow, which is always a sign that Carla is concentrating intensely.

She's so busy that she doesn't notice me taking two bottles of beer out of the big fridge next to the bar.

'Hey,' I say, putting the beer down on the bar.

She looks at me.

'Hello!'

Her brow smooths and then that smile comes. It's an incredible smile, and it takes me by surprise every time. As if I always forget overnight what Carla's smile can be like. She smiles with her whole body.

'Shall I take a beer out for you too?' I ask.

'Nah, leave it,' she says. 'I'd rather help Klatsche stack the beer crates for a bit.'

There's a clatter down in the cellar.

'I can do that,' I say. 'Your husband and the barbecue are waiting for you and the steak.'

Her smile dies out as quickly as it came. She's a master at that too. Quick changeovers.

She raises an eyebrow and blows out her cheeks.

'What's wrong?'

She washes her hands in the sink, takes a tea towel, dries them and says: 'Rocco wants kids.'

But as she says it, she looks more as though he's insisted that she conjure a monster factory out of thin air.

'And you don't want children,' I say, all lawyer, friend, woman.

She lights a cigarette.

'Nature's already made me that offer twice and I've turned it down both times. You know that.'

I nod and take a cigarette from her packet. Mine are outside with the man who wants a child with her.

'I always thought that was down to the fathers being the wrong guys,' I say.

Carla gives me a light.

'So did I. But now I realise that that wasn't the problem.'

We drag on our cigs.

'I don't want to be a mother, Chas. I'm not cut out for it.'

'I'm not cut out for it either, Carla.'

'Congrats. You're not the one married to a man who desperately wants to be a father.'

She looks at me; there's something glittering under her eyelids.

'What's brought this on so suddenly?'

She wipes her face.

'Damn it, smoke in my eyes.'

She takes a deep breath in and out, and then she cries anyway.

'Bloody idiot, he'll ruin everything.'

'Hold on,' I say and I open my beer and push it across to her.

She takes the bottle and drinks, looking me in the eye from the first sip to the last, and doesn't put the bottle down till it's empty.

OK.

That was clear.

Carla is a woman who makes no compromises. She thinks compromise is for cowards. I know that I can't afford to come out with anything like 'hold on,' again. Fuck holding on.

Either it'll sort itself out or it won't sort itself out. And it definitely won't sort itself out just because I stick my nose in.

Carla puts the empty beer bottle away and gets another from the fridge.

'Here,' she says and shoves the beer and the steak dish under my nose. 'Take him food and alcohol. That'll make him happy.'

What'll make him happy is you, I think – because I know it's true. But I don't say so. I jam the two bottles under my arm, take the dish and go back outside. Meanwhile, Carla climbs down to Klatsche in the cellar, which is really my job.

Outside, boom, the sun's gone down.

NOW

a wonky, battered drum
and a burning piece of fly-tipped junk
have become our sun.

SMOKE SIGNALS

Carla's standing next to Rocco by the barbecue.

I'm sitting next to Klatsche on the couch.

We're drinking beer.

Rocco's telling stories of his travels: he tells us about the Balkans, about France and Spain and Portugal; he tells us about North America and South America, about Morocco and Mozambique; and even though we all know the stories, they're new in one respect: suddenly, each story features children.

Carla stares into the embers. Rocco's stories go in her right ear and fall out of her left, and then she looks at the ground and thinks: would you look at that, there's something down there. But in the end, it's not actually all that interesting and she turns back to the embers.

I look at Klatsche, whose head is tipped right back as he stares into the darkening sky. Nothing happens when I look at him. I look at him and I'm not here at all.

The smoke that rises over the grilled meat settles down among us. As if someone were building walls.

I'll have a lamb's head soup, please.

BLACK BOX TWO

But then, alcohol eases a lot of things, even difficulties.

It's late at night and Carla and Rocco are half leaning, half lying, on the jukebox and I'm helping Klatsche behind the bar; it's just – or a bit – like old times, when things still made sense – at least these things here.

My phone chirps.

Ah.

Faller.

Hello, Hamburg.

Hello, Andalusia.

All OK?

All in the Blue Night.

Even the murder squad?

No. The murder squad's busy. I was there this afternoon.

Why?

Hit-and-run.

You've moved into hit-and-runs now?

Calabretta's moved into hit-and-runs. I've moved into coercion, false imprisonment and GBH.

How exactly?

Someone's torturing naked managers and then locking them up in cages.

Not bad. How far have you got?

Complex story. Wish you were here.

Wish you were HERE. It's still almost 20 degrees.

Snap!

No way.
Yes way.
Bloody climate change.

I put the phone aside and my arms round Klatsche. Perhaps I'm just imagining all this shit.

BIESENDORF
(1987)

They pulled him out of bed at night, again, and pushed him under the cold shower, like they do to all the new boys. But he's not new now. He joined them in year five. He was new then – and that was the first time they put him under the shower. Since then, they've put him under the shower almost every night. For five years, whenever they happen to feel like it, he's spent the night standing in cold water. And to stop him escaping into his nice, warm bed, they put the bed under the shower with him.

Schmidt, the Bean and Rösch.

It was just the three of them. And then a fourth was put in their room. With glasses, and smaller and thinner than the others. He didn't reply when anyone asked him anything. Perhaps they thought that if they put him in the shower night after night he might say something.

Now he's standing there again, still saying nothing.

But who could he talk to? Them? That's not what they want. At first, he kept thinking that, if he could just manage to talk to them, it might all stop, but he soon realised that they don't even want a reason to stop. To the teachers? Maybe he should talk to them? Or the housemasters? They keep their eyes and ears shut with beer. Kulmbacher beer. They start Kulmbaching in the mornings, everyone knows that. Nobody makes a secret of it. You need to be Kulmbached to cope with all the stuff in your head.

Hey, nobody's here by choice.

You hear the teachers talking over the Kulmbacher. They've all been transferred here because they've been sacked from better jobs.

The housemasters say nothing at all. There's even more beer flowing through them. They close the room doors in the evening and pull them open again in the morning without looking. Maybe they think it's better that way.

Nobody says anything about the black tooth either. It's black because they always aim footballs at it, Schmidt, the Bean and Rösch. And at his glasses too, of course. They play football three times a week. Have done for years. And if they miss the tooth or the glasses – which they do because, by year nine, if not earlier, it's not just the grown-ups drinking beer – they grab his face and shove it into a molehill. They say that's just what life's like.

And he doesn't even ask what life is really like.

Life is rosehip tea in the mornings.

With a milk roll.

Margarine.

Apricot jam.

Cervelat sausage and Edam.

Sometimes, if he's quick enough after breakfast, he manages to grab a toilet cubicle, ideally the one in the far corner – the one that always stinks so badly that nobody wants to go in there anyway. He locks himself in and waits until everyone's finished in the communal bathroom, until it's dead quiet. Only then does he venture out to the washbasins.

Those are the good days. On the bad days, Schmidt, the Bean and Rösch climb over the loo door and dunk his head in the bowl. Go on, have a wash, they say when they've finished, and he can still hear them laughing down the corridor.

In lessons, everyone has a Samsonite briefcase on the table. Open. That makes it harder for the teachers to see you. Schmidt, the Bean and Rösch draw pictures of him. With his head hacked off, or no legs. They fold the pictures into planes and throw them over to him. Once, he used to bother opening them. He doesn't any more. The others do it for him. So funny. The teachers say they didn't see any paper planes. They only see the sponges.

This is how it goes: you just walk up to the board, take the sponge, wet it, go back to your place and fire the thing at the board with a smack. Anyone can do that. Nothing happens if you throw a sponge. Schmidt has the best aim, the Bean has the hardest throw and, lately, Rösch has taken to throwing them at the window next to the teacher's desk.

Once, a new teacher asked the Bean the meaning of this. The Bean asked what the hell was it to him? Because that's the standard answer to a teacher's questions. So the teacher smacked the Bean one. The Bean stood up and smacked the teacher one, but with his fist. Generally, if there's a fist fight between teachers and pupils, it's the teachers who end up having to hit back if they don't want to go down. Basically, no one would be surprised if the occasional teacher got put under the shower at night too.

Because in the end, no one cares. It's like little Böhringer: his dad's got that fur shop in central Nuremberg. One day, the boy'll take it over, with or without qualifications. So long as he's away for long enough that his dad can run the business and his mum can play tennis. But the being-away works out well enough. Old man Böhringer's paying for it.

Lunch is the same every week.

Monday is baked rice.

Tuesday is omelette.

Wednesday is mince soup.

Thursday is Pichelsteiner stew

Friday is fried herring.

The fried herring is the worst; nobody can eat that. Although, one Friday, the Bean ate all the fried herring, and I'll give you three guesses who had to pay him a crate of Kulmbacher for that: Four-Eyes. Unfortunately, he didn't have the money for a crate of beer. So Schmidt and Rösch lent him the money. He had to sign IOUs for it. He could work them off with compulsory labour, mostly during the study period after lunch. Then he had to do homework for three.

The IOUs have been worked off, but the homework carries on.

It's just such a nice tradition, as Schmidt always says when he pushes his geography book over to him.

Sometimes, in the evening, he can't stand it any longer and he drinks himself unconscious on Kulmbacher. In the morning, when he wakes up, he's got burns from their cigarettes on his arms, and now and again there's one on his forehead. And everyone finds it hilarious.

The only one who doesn't find these things funny is Yeller. Yeller is the caretaker. Apparently, he was once the head. Nobody knows why he stopped being head and became caretaker instead. Yeller lives in a funny house alongside the school. His name isn't actually Yeller but something else, but he has such hideous yellow teeth that everyone calls him Yeller.

And they hate him because he doesn't leave them in peace. Because he doesn't just put up with all their shit. The Night of Broken Glass, for instance – that rankles with him. The other adults always bow out very early in the day, heading for the Kulmbacher; on the dot of sunset they stop noticing a thing, and in November that's around five. So it kicks off around seven or half past, just after dinner. Anything that can smash gets thrown out of the windows. Glasses, bottles, whole crates of beer. The Bean ripped out a washbasin once, and, once, even a toilet. Out they go.

Let Yeller sweep it up tomorrow.

One Night of Broken Glass, Schmidt broke into the locked book-case in the staffroom and threw the books out of the window. But he set them on fire first. He filled the empty cupboard with the broken chairs lying around the corridors.

Every time there's a Night of Broken Glass, Yeller grumbles that he didn't board up his parents' shop on the Nazi Kristallnacht just to have to deal with a crappy Night of Broken Crockery here.

There was a single occasion when two people were kicked out of school, but that wasn't because of the Night of Broken Glass. What they did was bigger still, and Schmidt, the Bean and Rösch, and everyone else, are still talking about it.

One night, these two broke into a car dealership and nicked a Fiat. Then they pulled a cigarette machine off the wall. With the dough in their pockets, they drove to the festival in Nuremberg. Where they found two girls. They filled them up with gin, and then, in the car, they did anything you can think of that you can do to girls with two litres of gin in their bloodstreams.

When they tried to get back into the school at the crack of dawn, they were so pissed they got caught in the barbed wire that Yeller had fenced his house in with. But Yeller didn't just have barbed wire. Yeller also had a shotgun.

Anyway, *they* were kicked out.

The music teacher is sitting at the piano in the music room, playing. They're throwing small change at him. When the coins skip onto the piano they clink. Somebody's turned the crucifix above the piano upside-down.

Watch out, says Schmidt, and there's no way of knowing exactly who he's addressing. Watch out or you might end up hanging upside-down too.

ENGINE NOISES

Saturday evening and I'm doing something pretty nuts.

I'm lying on the sofa. The sofa doesn't know what's happening to it, and every ten minutes or so it pinches me in the side. But maybe the pinch has more to do with me being in my mid-forties. Anyway, overall, it's surprisingly OK for both of us.

I'm smoking, drinking a bottle of white wine and looking through the open window at the couple arguing in the loft apartment opposite, and at the sky. I didn't feel like going out. I felt like thinking. And having sole responsibility for the hangover I'll be sporting tomorrow.

Things to think about:

1. The business with Klatsche.
2. The fact that these three publishing types have clearly always done everything together, from school through to their management jobs, yet they really don't seem like the kind of people who'd find stuff like that important.

I've been trying to think about Klatsche for an hour now. I haven't got very far. It seems to me that we've been not-a-couple for almost ten years, that, on the whole, it's been more difficult than easy for both of us, and that that's never been down to him. That's the best I can do. But it's bullshit thinking about that stuff anyway. Or maybe it isn't.

The couple opposite are getting down to the nitty-gritty. She throws a plate at the wall and, if I'm not mistaken, the missile misses his head by a hair's breadth. He bangs the flat door shut and runs down the stairs. I sometimes meet him down at the kiosk when we're both buying cigarettes or beer. I wonder how much longer that will last. This is the third time this month that he's walked out, slamming the door. Six months ago, when they had both just moved in, they kept walking around the flat naked, after sex on the kitchen table. Living together isn't good for them.

I top myself up and wonder what Sebastian Schmidt's doing at the moment, whether he's drinking wine too, round the fire with his wife, and whether she's eating chocolate with it again, and whether she knows that her husband ran someone down, killing her outright.

Then my phone rings.

It's Stepanovic.

He's outdoors, maybe by the water – I can hear gulls. And a dull roar. Engine noises.

'Where are you?' I ask.

'On a ferry across the Elbe, what about you?'

'At home.'

'Not very glamorous.'

'So what?'

'Hang on a second, I've dropped my cigarette in the river.'

He lights another, and so do I.

'I'm back,' he says. 'Will you come down to Bavaria with me on Monday?'

'What would I do in Bavaria?'

'I want a look at the boarding school those three gentlemen were at. And four eyes are better than two.'

'I don't know.'

I don't want to go to Bavaria.

'Sahin and the guys are needed here – they're up to their eyeballs in witness statements.'

'I really don't know.'

We hardly know each other. I don't like travelling with someone I don't know to a strange place.

'Get a grip, Riley. Dr Kolb told me yesterday evening that you like the odd trip out. And that it wouldn't be a problem.'

'You didn't even want to come for a beer with me yesterday.'

'What do you mean by that?'

'You know.'

We smoke and think about it.

'OK, listen,' he says. 'We'll go. I'll pick you up on Monday morning, early. Six OK?'

I say: 'Half past.'

START BUYING MAKE-UP

It's early. The roads are empty. The country's racing by – we're not far from Hanover now. Misty, flat Lower Saxony everywhere. Help.

'Coffee?'

I've almost forgotten that Stepanovic is sitting beside me. I've almost forgotten anyone's driving the car. Too long looking out of the window: brain fallen out.

'I could,' I say.

'I should,' he says. 'If I don't get caffeine soon, we'll be in the central reservation before long.'

The car slows down. I find myself yawning and stretch my arms up to the roof. Out of the corner of my eye, I see Stepanovic smile.

'You're easy company, Riley.'

'I have my moments.'

'I know.'

'How do you know?'

'I know women.'

He parks in a space right in front of the toilets.

'Good idea,' I say.

'I know women,' he repeats.

As I wash my hands, I make the mistake of looking in the mirror. My black T-shirt is not only stretched rather brashly over my breasts, but also totally crumpled. As if I've slept in it. My pale coat is in an equally mistreated state. My hair is hanging down over my face; it's too long and needs a cut. I stroke it back behind my ears. You can see the black circles under my eyes better that way. Hell. I'm really nothing to write home about. I look like a half-demolished house.

If I'm honest, lately I look like this all the time. I have no idea what Klatsche wants from me any more; in fact, I have more of an idea that he doesn't want anything from me any longer. But maybe I don't want anything from him any longer either.

For God's sake.

I turn on the cold tap and hold my face under it. Carla's been saying for some time that I really ought to start buying make-up.

The coffee that Stepanovic puts in front of me is hot and black. I tip too much sugar into it.

'What's up with you anyway, Riley?'

'Why should anything be up?'

'Well, in general. I look at you and can't see through at all.'

'That's normal,' I say, 'I'm like that too.'

'With yourself or other people?'

'With everyone. Aren't you?'

'No,' he says. 'Normally I can get a pretty good idea of people. And when I look in the mirror, I see someone who I know through and through.' He slurps down a gulp of coffee. 'And who, if you're being generous, looks like he used to play for Croatia.'

'You always know who you are?'

'Sure.'

So. That 'sure' was so deeply Frankfurterish that I absolutely have to ask.

'Where did you grow up?'

'Frankfurt. Sachsenhausen. Why?'

'Just wondered,' I say, but then I add: 'Me too.'

'I see,' he says, and looks at me like that's really true.

He finishes his coffee, I drink mine, we go for a smoke and don't say anything else for quite a long time.

Somewhere around Kassel I feel a bit sick.

Just before the A5 heads off towards Frankfurt, my stomach rumbles. The man behind the wheel says: 'I'm starving too. Will a sandwich do, or do you need a restaurant?'

'A cheese sandwich would do.'

'A cheese sandwich would be really great right now,' he says. 'Maybe with a nice, cool apple juice?'

'Cheese sandwich and apple juice,' I say. 'Killer combo.'

'Let's do that.'

I look sideways at him.

He notices me looking.

'I look damn fine behind the wheel, huh? I should have been a racing driver.'

He lays his arm behind my headrest, looks at me, as if we were on the screen, and moves over to the right – rather impetuously for my taste; especially now that the motorway's filled up.

Up ahead is our nearest service station.

CIGARETTES AS A WEAPON

There aren't any cheese sandwiches, there are only cheese rolls. It's not the same, but it'll do.

'What do you reckon is waiting for us down there?' I ask.

'In Biesendorf?'

He shrugs, bites into his roll and chews. Then he spreads out his long arms and says: 'Germany. Germany's waiting for us.'

He smiles and puts his head on one side; he does things with his face that make him look like a nineties' TV host.

'As a kid, I was always scared of ending up in a boarding school one day,' I say.

'My parents sometimes threatened me with that too, and, actually, I found the idea quite exciting,' he says. 'But they could never have afforded it.'

'What did your parents do?'

'We had a little Yugoslavian snack bar. Right behind Frankfurt-Süd station. They shifted huge portions of *cevapcici* with red rice every day. Have you ever tried it?'

'I'm not really the mince type.'

'What type are you then?'

'The cheese sandwich type.'

'What else?'

'Soused herring.'

'I don't mean the food.'

'Oh, don't start that again.'

'C'mon, Riley, I just want to get to know you. We're working together.'

I bite into my cheese roll and chew. It tastes stodgy. I wash it down with apple juice.

OK, then. Right.

'I'm the type who generally gets the feeling that something isn't right. I'm the type who feels the cold easily. I'm the type who's rarely doing particularly well unless she's by the sea. I'm the type who drowns her troubles in alcohol and then smokes them out with cigarettes. I'm the type who didn't want to be at home anywhere but then put down roots anyway, and I'm the type who feels unsettled by that. I'm easily unsettled anyway, even if I don't look like it. I'm the type who finds that all the injustice in the world goes down like a bucket of cold sick.'

I put my roll down.

'And I'm the type who doesn't like rolls and is going for a pee.'

I leave him and the stodgy roll at the sticky table and vanish towards the loo to hide for a while because, obviously, I'm regretting my outburst exactly two seconds later. But if you ask, you get answers.

On the way back, I stop at the kiosk and buy cigarettes, which I lay on the table in front of Stepanovic as if they were a weapon. Beats me why I think this gesture will impress him, why I even feel the need to impress him, but it just seems that way to me.

He drinks his apple juice, puts down the bottle, gives me a crooked grin and says: 'Come on, Riley, let's get going.'

We sit in the Mercedes again. He starts the engine and drives off with a squeal of tyres.

'Well, slap my lederhosen, I haven't been to Bavaria for years.'

I've never been to Bavaria, I think, which is really almost scandalous, given that I grew up practically next door.

Half an hour later, as if someone had flicked a switch, the landscape becomes both very hilly and far too cute for my tastes.

TUSCANY, MY ARSE

There's a carved wooden village sign as you drive into the place. The sign says that this is the 'Franconian Tuscany', which is pretty close to being a very bad joke. In Tuscany, there'd be people on the streets and in the squares: they'd be chatting, they'd be laughing, they'd be alive. In Biesendorf, nothing, absolutely nothing, is like Tuscany, except possibly the fact that this backwater is set in a hilly landscape. And, OK, there are vines on the slopes.

But I've never seen so many rolling shutters in all my life. Most of the shutters are down. In the middle of the day.

Stepanovic parks the Mercedes behind a sort of village square. In the centre is a beautiful old fountain, freshly renovated, with a golden statue of a saint at the top. But there's no water. As if the fountain were fake. On the other side of the street there's an inn. The inn is called The Final Cut.

We get out.

'If that's the only restaurant here,' I say, 'I'm not eating anything.'

'I'll shoot you a wild boar,' says Stepanovic, locking the car. 'But let's go for a bit of a walk first.'

I look left, towards a rare house without rolling barricades lowered in front of its windows. The curtain moves. And then suddenly it isn't moving any more. We walk down the main street, which snakes through the village. We only catch sight of a few people, and they're sitting in cars. There's nobody on foot. We pass two butcher's shops, which are offering Bavarian *leberkäse* burgers, Hawaiian burgers and lasagne. Pass three barber's shops that only cut men's hair. Pass at least six snack bars. There are kebabs, currywurst, noodles. The houses on the main road look deserted; some have lost their doorbell name-plates, but some, astonishingly, do have them.

There are midges whirring over the street; it's humid.

At the end of the road, there's a supermarket with a huge poster slapped up by the entrance: 'Saturday! Grand Opening of the New Supermarket Car Park! With Free Bubbly! And the Mayor!'

Stepanovic stops by the banner.

'Can we stay till Saturday?'

Somehow, I can't shake off the feeling that this man would even turn the last cartload of dung into a joke.

'This is an awful place,' I say.

'Hey, listen, this is the Franconian Tuscany.'

'Tuscany, my arse.'

We sit on a bench and smoke.

'Maybe you're not such easy company, Riley. You don't even want to join the mayor in wetting the head of the new supermarket car park.'

'I said I have my moments. Where is this stupid school, anyway?'

He uses his cigarette to point towards a tree-covered hill at the far end of the main road.

'Somewhere up there. We're being watched, by the way.'

True. The curtains behind the few non-barricaded windows nearby are moving in that scurrying way again.

I make a point of dropping my cigarette on the pavement. I really am uneasy.

BUT WITH A LITTLE ILL WILL, YOU COULD THINK THAT THERE'S SOMEONE LYING BEHIND THE BROKEN WINDOWS, WHO'S BEEN ROTTING IN THERE FOR YEARS

'This is the Bavaria I know,' says Stepanovic. 'An undiluted mixture of suspicion and aggression.'

A middle-aged man in a red tracksuit has actually just tried to chase us off the school grounds with a stick; Stepanovic only just managed to whip out his ID before the guy clobbered him. Now he seems to have vanished off the face of the Earth. He's probably informing the entire staff that the police are here. I bet he's the PE teacher.

We start by looking at the place from the outside. The large building to the left must be the school; there's a playground in front of it and a sports field next to that. To our right is a squat, cowering, two-storey building. Through the tilted windows, I can see bunkbeds, a few wardrobes, tables and chairs, and a shared bathroom. A little further on, there's a small house that threatens to collapse in on itself the minute you get too close. The windows are smashed, the roof has holes in it, the front door is askew. As if it had just been left behind, as if the resident has gone and has never looked back. But with a little ill will, you could think that there's someone lying behind the broken windows, someone who's been quietly rotting in there for years.

A few trees and bushes and hedges are dotted around here and there; here and there, there are views of Biesendorf, of red tiled roofs and an onion-topped church tower. From above, it looks almost like a postcard.

'"Little Darkling in late summer",' I say.

'What?'

Stepanovic is holding his right eye shut, scanning the area with just his left.

'Never mind.'

There's a strange silence lying over the school and the boarding house. As if there were nobody here, even though you know that there must be someone here.

Then the double door to the school building opens and out comes a man of middling height with middling-brown hair and a pale, badly fitting suit. He's wearing walking shoes. His eyebrows are the short type that kink in the middle. He walks towards us with slightly overlong steps; his facial expression veers between unfriendly and outraged.

'Yes? Can I help? You wanted to speak to me?'

I wouldn't necessarily put it quite like that, I think, but Stepanovic says: 'Yes. Ivo Stepanovic, SCO Hamburg.' And, with a look in my direction: 'Chastity Riley, the Public Prosecutor for the case.'

'SCO Hamburg? What do you want from us?'

I hold out my hand.

'What was your name again?'

'Fischer,' he says, giving me a weedy handshake. 'Siegfried Fischer. I am the head of this establishment.'

Establishment. You might as well say 'institution'.

'Nice of you to make time for us, Mr Fischer,' says Stepanovic, walking forcefully towards the school. 'Could we have a quick chat in your office?'

Sometimes he has this way of smiling away everything in his path.

Fischer seems to be taken by surprise by so much gushing audacity. He murmurs, 'Yes, of course,' and then trots behind Stepanovic, robbed of all his outrage.

Inside the school, it smells of something with rice.

There are corridors.

There are stairs.

There's grey lino and schoolwork in display cases.

Everything's in good nick, yet it's also as though things are cleaned too often.

Fischer climbs a wide staircase; we follow. His office is on the first floor, at the end of a long corridor. There's a big desk, two cupboards, a bookcase, a window with a view of Biesendorf framed by two houseplants. In the corner, next to the window, there's a small round table with four chairs.

The headteacher speaks: 'Take a seat.'

He waves towards the seating area. We sit down and wait, and try not to take the missing 'please' personally. Fischer stands by his desk, primly pushing a few things around. Perhaps he can't help it, perhaps he can't say 'please', and perhaps he has to keep all his guests waiting. As if everyone who comes into this room were a pupil who's been up to something.

Then so be it.

One of the first things that I learnt from Faller about good policing was this: always start by waiting until people can't stand the silence and start talking.

Then ask the right questions.

DO YOU LIVE HERE?

'The eighties? There's nobody left from that time.'

'Not a single teacher who was still young then?'

Fischer shakes his head.

'The school was restructured in the late nineties. We now focus wholly on business studies. Consequently, there were a lot of staff changes.'

'So, the entire staff changed?'

Fischer nods. 'Basically, yes. But it was done in a socially sustainable way. Through semi-retirement, early retirement and secondments.'

Fischer crosses his arms over his chest and raises his chin. Stepanovic takes notes. He is just as aware as I am that Fischer has no intention of revealing anything close to what happened here back then.

'What about the caretaker from those days?' I ask.

'He died.'

'When did he die?'

'A couple of years ago,' says Fischer. 'He drove his Opel into a tree. He was a kind of odd-job man and he lived in the caretaker's house here on site. I kept trying to persuade him to stop driving once he was in his nineties, but he would never listen to anyone, as usual.'

'And the current caretaker doesn't live here?' I ask.

'Nope,' says Fischer, trotting out a cold, bleating laugh. 'He doesn't live here.'

'Do you live here then?'

The laugh is gone again.

'Heaven forbid. I live with my family in Würzburg.'

'We need the school files,' says Stepanovic, looking up from his notes. 'From 1980 to the mid-nineties.'

'Why?' asks Fischer.

'We need information about that period. About pupils, teachers, other staff,' says Stepanovic. 'And if we can't get that here, we'll just have to fight our way through the relevant files.'

'I haven't got the files,' says Fisher.

Of course not, I think.

'They're held by the Board of Education in Nuremberg.'

The main thing is that he has nothing to do with anything.

I'm bloody sick of people like that.

I TOLD THE CLEANING LADY NOT TO COME

We stroll through the side streets. Some of the houses look almost like old farms, with new buildings between them that have kept growing too tall. There's a stream flowing between the houses, and nobody's straightened it out yet, which makes a nice change. There are arrangements of park benches in the bends and on the small, ivy-covered bridges. As if there were actually people on the street here, wanting to sit down.

'We'll start by looking for somewhere to sleep,' says Stepanovic.

'I'd rather sleep in the car than in the Final Cut,' I say.

'Nobody intends to force a room in the Final Cut on you.'

'Have you seen any alternative? There were only butchers and food joints.'

'We'll find something,' he says, stopping by an old whitewashed house with large windows.

'I believe you,' I say and at exactly the same moment, I grasp the meaning of the sign on the door, which says, in red block capitals:

THIS PRACTICE WILL REMAIN CLOSED UNTIL THE MAYOR STOPS FUCKING MY WIFE.

Beside it, on a little silver plaque is an inscription in subtle black script:

Dr Johannes Wollmann, GP.

'The doctor appears to be an outspoken gentleman,' says Stepanovic with a somewhat sleazy grin.

'He doesn't seem like a mystery-monger at any rate,' I say. 'We should speak to Johannes Wollman, don't you think?'

'Definitely.'

Stepanovic rings the bell.

After a while, the door opens.

Standing in the doorframe is a blond man in jeans and a polo shirt, whose skin tone suggests that he spends most of his time on the tennis court.

'Dr Wollmann?' I ask.

'Yes. Can I help you?'

'My name is Chastity Riley. I'm a public prosecutor in Hamburg. This is Ivo Stepanovic from the SCO. Can you spare us a few minutes?'

'What do you want to ask me?'

He leans against the doorframe and looks us over; he looks more amused than surprised.

'We'd like to speak to you about the boarding school on the hill,' I say.

'Why me?'

'Simply because we've got to start somewhere,' says Stepanovic. 'And so far, we haven't had much luck, either here in the village or up at the school.'

'I see,' says Wollmann, giving us a broad smile. 'This place is quite the shithole. Nobody talks to anyone.' He takes a step to the side, freeing up the doorway. 'Come in.'

His surgery is bright and modern, with mountains of dust everywhere.

'Please excuse the look of the place,' he says. 'I told the cleaning lady not to come when I shut up surgery.'

'When was that?' I ask.

'Three months ago.'

'And that sign's been on the door ever since?'

'Yes,' he says, kicking open the door to his consultation room. 'I just didn't feel like sitting quietly and letting people take the piss.'

HOW YOU FILL THE TOES OF FOOTBALL BOOTS WITH DRAWING PINS

Well, fancy that: once you get out of that miserable place, this is actually a very beautiful area. We're sitting on the terrace of a country hotel a few kilometres south of Biesendorf, and smoking. There's a soft, warm wind blowing and even a bit of sunshine still. Beyond the terrace flows the obligatory country hotel stream; an old millwheel rattles. The house has wild vines growing up the walls and, here and there, the leaves are already starting to turn red. Our rooms are on the second floor; we've got one each with a view of the hills.

Dr Wollman has arranged to meet us for an early-evening dinner – he had to rush off to an appointment at the golf course that afternoon. He said he'd been to the school himself, and we could ask him whatever we liked; he had nothing left to lose here. He'd probably close the practice permanently anyway soon; his wife and the mayor were playing at happy couples, and he'd had it up to here with all that shit.

On the way back to Stepanovic's car, we realise the point of the park benches all over the place. They're the youth centres. Where you hang out after school. Where you stand around, smoke and hurl abuse at innocent visitors from Hamburg who walk past unawares. Enquiries as to what we are looking at are followed by the suggestion that we go and fuck ourselves.

Fresh light dawns: no wonder there's nobody out for a little stroll around here.

Dr Wollmann arrives on the dot of six. He orders a bottle of local wine and starts talking. He's actually from Nuremberg, but he met his wife here in Biesendorf while he was still at school. He opted for civilian national service, came back after a couple of years, married her, and eventually took over her father's GP practice. And then, one day, the shit with the mayor happened.

'The guy's a massive arsehole.'

We raise our glasses and drink. A woodpigeon whirrs over our heads.

'Do you mind telling us how old you are?' asks Stepanovic.

'Forty-seven. Why?'

'We're interested in the school in the eighties.'

'Ask away, then,' he says. 'That's my era.'

Stepanovic leans back and looks at Wollmann.

'Do the names Tobias Rösch, Leonhard Bohnsen and Sebastian Schmidt mean anything to you?'

Dr Wollmann thinks. Drinks wine. Looks at the menu. Beckons the waitress over.

'Shouldn't we order first?'

He goes for wild boar, Stepanovic opts for steak, and I have the trout.

And another bottle of wine, please.

Once the bottle's standing open on the table, Wollmann says: 'Yes, actually, I remember that gang pretty well.'

'Why them in particular?' I ask, lighting a cigarette.

Stepanovic would like one too. Gets one. Dr Wollmann too.

'They were no worse and no better than the rest of us,' he says. 'Apart from that one thing, maybe. That was quite exceptionally bad.'

We draw the smoke down into our lungs almost simultaneously. We sound like a factory.

'I was two years above them, so it's surprising that I knew about it at all. But it wasn't something you could miss.'

Spit it out, man.

'At first there were just the three of them sharing a room. But a fourth boy was put in with them six months later.'

'In the middle of the school year?' I ask.

'That wasn't particularly unusual,' he says. 'It's not your classic posh boarding school. There are the sons of relatively well-off parents – businessmen, lawyers, upper middle class. And boys from the village. And every year has a good handful of kids from troubled backgrounds, taken from their families by social services and shoved into Biesendorf School to be looked after.'

'An explosive mixture,' says Stepanovic.

'Right,' says Wollmann. 'So, people would fight back on principle if a teacher thought he'd get results by boxing ears. Every day was a long stream of disrespect and provocation.'

'What happened to this fourth boy?' I ask.

Wollmann smokes, looks up at the sky. A doctor who smokes is always a special case, I think.

'He suffered. From the very first day. They screwed him over in any way they could think of. That's not unheard of in boarding schools, but it seemed to me from the outset that they absolutely needed somebody to tyrannise, or they'd have burst. Even in year five, they were like that. Especially Sebastian. He was the ringleader. He decided what to do, and then Tobi and Leo did it. And if they couldn't find a pupil to torment, they'd pick on one of the weaker teachers.'

'What was the fourth boy's name?' asks Stepanovic.

Wollmann drags on his cigarette and runs his finger round the rim of his wineglass. There's a very delicate, singing sound, if you listen carefully.

'Schmidt's Cat.'

'Sorry?' I ask.

'That's what everyone called him,' says Wollmann. 'Even the teachers.' He takes a sip of wine. 'I have no idea what his actual name was.'

'We need those damn files,' I say.

'The school board's in Nuremberg,' says Wollmann.

'We called them this afternoon,' I say. 'Nobody there. Public bodies like to knock off early. We'll fix them first thing tomorrow.'

Stepanovic fumbles with his top shirt button and undoes it. It's still bloody hot.

'What did Schmidt, Bohnsen and Rösch do to this boy?'

'Everything painful and humiliating,' says Wollmann.

But once he's started listing a few things, I'd rather not listen too carefully. I hope Stepanovic is taking it all in.

'Why are you interested in all this anyway? What's happened?' asks Wollman, after he's described in detail how you fill the toes of football boots with drawing pins, making quite sure that the owner of the boots doesn't notice until the tacks are already under his nails.

Stepanovic stubs out his cigarette.

'First Bohnsen and then Rösch were victims of violent assaults. We're looking into their backgrounds.'

'Are they still hanging around together?' asks Dr Wollmann, and judging by his wry expression, he finds that just as contemptible as I did when I first heard about it.

'They work for the same company,' says Stepanovic. 'And Sebastian Schmidt is their boss.'

'That doesn't surprise me in the least. And, do you know what? If you'd told me thirty years ago that it would turn out like that, I wouldn't have been surprised then either. It wouldn't really surprise me if I heard it about any of us. When you think about it all it's kind of outrageous.'

The food arrives. Enormous plates with enormous portions. Country hotel style.

'This fourth boy, Schmidt's Cat,' I say, 'you don't happen to know what he's doing now?'

Wollmann cuts off a piece of his roast wild boar and sticks it in his mouth. Stepanovic tears at his steak with knife and fork. I fillet my trout.

'When he was fifteen, or thereabouts, Schmidt's Cat went into hospital and never came back to school,' says Wollmann. 'But I can't remember exactly when it was.'

'So, what happened?' asks Stepanovic, chewing.

'There was a rumour that he'd slit his wrists. But the teachers didn't discuss it with us.'

'So nobody at the school knew precisely why the boy suddenly left?' I ask.

'Exactly.'

'You never heard anything else?'

'Never.'

'Can you think of anybody,' says Stepanovic, 'who might know anything?'

Wollmann eats more wild boar and thinks.

'Old Fuchs, maybe.'

'Who is that?' I ask.

'Quirin Fuchs's father. Schmidt's Cat did have a friend at the school, but only one: Quirin. Weird kid; you'd probably call him a nerd nowadays.'

'And his father lives in Biesendorf?'

'Yeah. Quirin was a dumpster.'

'A what?' asks Stepanovic.

'There were the boarders and the dumpsters,' says Wollmann. 'Dumpsters were the ones who lived with their parents and only came up to the school for lessons. Lowest rank in the hierarchy.' He crams his last large piece of roast boar into his mouth and chews. 'But if you ask me, Quirin is the only person who might know what happened to Schmidt's Cat when he left.'

He places his cutlery on the plate and pushes it aside. I pour more wine.

Dr Wollmann slides down a bit in his chair, shakes his head and seems to be pondering.

Then he says: 'The two of them spent hours playing some stupid dice game. Might have been a role-playing game. Anyway, they were constantly at this table in the common room, with all sorts of bits of paper and figures, pretending to be someone else.'

'It all sounds to me like Schmidt's Cat and Quirin Fuchs were the perfect victims,' says Stepanovic.

'Yup,' says Wollmann, 'they were top-class victims. But if it hadn't been those two, it would have been someone else. Can you imagine what goes on in a place like that with no women, no girls? In a closed system made up of maybe a hundred and eighty boys? Before, during and after puberty? And then there are maybe twenty men in charge of the whole thing. At a rough estimate, that's two hundred overloaded guys.'

'Somehow I don't want to imagine it,' I say.

'It's an empathy-free zone,' says Wollmann. 'There's no compassion and there's no one to say that this or that is wrong. The boys arrive after primary school. They're ten or eleven. Over the next few years, you either have to grow a very thick skin around your heart, or else you can just chuck it away.'

'What happened to *your* heart?' asks Stepanovic, and I feel my own do a little jump as he asks the question.

Wollmann takes a big gulp from his wineglass.

'I can't tell you. I've never dared think about it. And when my mood shifts, I head for the golf course.'

By this time, Stepanovic and I have also finished our meals. The waitress clears away. I hand out cigarettes.

'Where does this old Mr Fuchs live?' asks Stepanovic.

'I've got his address in my patient files. Call tomorrow morning and I'll give it to you. But be nice to the man; he doesn't have it easy. His wife died young and he's grown a bit odder every year since.'

Stepanovic raises his hands and tries to look like a wise, old sea captain.

'Do you get the impression we're not nice?'

Wollmann smiles. Stepanovic gives him a light and then me. How quickly people become allies.

'Do you happen to know anything about the big staff changes in the late nineties?' I ask. 'The headteacher told us that practically all the teachers were switched and the place turned into a business school. Was there any particular reason why that happened? Was there a scandal?'

'You mean the usual abuse cases?'

'For example.'

Wollmann shook his head.

'It was much more banal. Eventually, everyone around here knew what conditions were like in the school; everyone knew that the place had gone to the dogs. So the education minister went on a quality drive, and they had to comply or they'd have shut the joint down. They lost their clientele because everyone who could even remotely afford it sent their kids to rich-folks' boarding schools, or actually looked after them at home. So, instead of just having teachers who'd been transferred there for disciplinary reasons, they wanted to attract really highly trained educationalists with salaries to match. To improve the school's reputation, and probably also to gradually nudge it towards being a hot-house for the elite.'

'And?' asks Stepanovic. 'Did it work?'

Dr Wollmann looks at us, drains his glass and laughs himself silly.

COUNTRY STUFF

The honest doctor made tracks during the third bottle of Franconian, after which, Stepanovic and I had devoted ourselves to the Müller-Thurgau.

'Did you know that this is the wine that Charles Bukowski drank himself unconscious on, the time he visited Hamburg in the seventies?'

'No,' I say, 'I didn't know that. But it's good that you know stuff like that.'

'Artistic soul,' he says.

'Seriously?'

'Well kind of. Maybe that's more a drinker's soul speaking. I like Bukowski. How about you? What do you like?'

'The wine isn't bad.'

We're sitting on a bench outside our country hotel. All the other guests have gone or are in bed. All the lights are off, only the stars are on.

'Wow, look at all the stars,' I say for want of anything better.

'D'you see the moon last week, Chas?'

Stepanovic slips deeper into the bench, takes a swig from the umpteenth bottle of Müller-Thurgau, passes it to me, rests his hands in his lap and his head on the backrest and shuts his eyes. If I want to keep our relationship professional, I've got to tackle him now. But hey, I could actually make friends with someone in my middle age.

'I did,' I say. 'It blew me away.'

Quite how, I don't say. You don't have to let your friends in on everything right away.

'I sat up by the window half the night, listening to music,' he says. 'Do you like music?'

'Only in bars,' I say.

'And what do you listen to then?'

He really means it about getting to know each other. I swig from the bottle.

'Johnny Cash, Screaming Jay Hawkins, country stuff.' OK, now for it: 'How about you, Ivo?'

So much bourgeois affinity makes me instantly dizzy. I mean: we're talking about music. We were just discussing Bukowski. Any minute we'll be booking theatre tickets for next weekend.

'Everything,' he says.

'Everything?'

'Everything.'

He lays his arm along the back of the bench, behind me, turns towards me, glances up at the starry sky again, and then he gives me that look.

Uh, no.

You can forget that, mate.

MELON WOULD BE BETTER

Put it like this: more than three bottles of Müller-Thurgau equals headache. And Dr Wollmann is, at least in this respect, cleverer than us.

'But the sky was nuts,' says Stepanovic as we sit down to breakfast and force ourselves to eat a little scrambled egg. This is like a holiday at rock bottom.

'I rang Wollmann,' I say, pushing away the plate of egg. Maybe a slice of melon would be better. There's always melon in hotels. 'This Quirin Fuchs' father doesn't live far from his surgery.'

'Give me half an hour, Chas, and I'll call the education department in Nuremberg and drive us over to old Mr Fuchs.'

Oh yeah. We're mates, Ivo and me.

Later, when we're sitting in the car, I wish we could go back to our old professional terms, or alternatively that I could get on to the next bottle of Müller-Thurgau.

THE BOY DIED

The house is one of the long-abandoned-looking ones, and Alfons Fuchs is pretty much the same. He has only a small cluster of grey hair left – a few strands on his head, a few strands on his chin. He's wearing a faded old-man shirt, jeans that are too big and held up by a cracked, brown leather belt, and a dark-green cardigan.

Nobody cares, that's plain to see.

'Mr Fuchs?'

His expression is as frayed as his cardigan. He nods.

Stepanovic shows him his ID and gives him a very gentle smile. Like me, he seems to feel that this old man might crumble into dust if the wind caught him full in the face.

'We've come from Hamburg,' I say. 'And we'd like to speak to you about a school friend of your son's. Could you spare us a moment?'

He looks us both over from top to toe, looks at us very closely indeed. Faces, shirts, trousers, boots. It takes a while. Then he turns around and shuffles into the house.

'Come in.'

He speaks more to the dark hallway than to us.

We're invited to take a seat on the three-piece suite in the living room. A three-seater, a two-seater, an armchair, all in claret. And from the early eighties, I reckon. Standing on the coffee table, which has, over the years, found its way away from the sofas and over to the armchair, is a bottle of beer. The TV's on. Some daytime programme in which heavily made-up people are having breakfast. On the sideboard by the TV there are countless pictures of a boy and a woman. The boy is dark blond, tall and gangling; his mouth looks as though he has a few more teeth than other people. His expression is shrewd but closed. The pretty, plumpish woman is laughing in all the photos, and she's no older than forty in any of them.

Fuchs switches off the box, sits down in the armchair and looks at us.

'We would like to know a little more about a school friend of your son, Quirin,' says Stepanovic. 'Unfortunately, we don't even know his name just at the moment.'

'Which school do you mean?'

'The boarding school.'

'Quirin only had the one friend there.'

'Do you know his name?'

He takes a swig of beer and looks out of the window.

'Wait a bit.'

We wait.

'Cat. He was called Cat.'

'He wasn't called Cat,' I say, realising that the thread of my patience is suddenly at snapping point. 'He must have had a proper name. First name, surname, something of that sort.'

'I can't help you there.'

'Do you know anything else about the boy?' I ask, trying to turn down the heat under my impatience.

'It was sad,' says Fuchs. 'It was very sad when he suddenly went into hospital, and then I never saw him here again. Quirin didn't tell me anything. I think the boy died.'

'Why do you think that?' I ask.

'That's how it felt.'

'Can you tell us where we can find your son?' asks Stepanovic. 'Perhaps he knows something more.'

'My son lives in Hamburg,' says Fuchs, throwing us a look as if he's really given us something to think about.

'In Hamburg?' I ask.

'Yes,' he says, crossing his legs with an air of satisfaction. 'The place you come from.'

Stepanovic and I glance at each other. He's probably thinking exactly what I'm thinking. That at this moment, a whole new light is worming in through the greyed curtains and cautiously resting on our case.

'What does your son do in Hamburg, then?' Stepanovic asks, pulling out his notebook.

If the police gets out its notebook, things are getting serious, I know that. Fuchs doesn't know that; he just seems pleased that somebody's asked for once. He chatters merrily on about it.

'Something to do with computers. Quirin was always good with computers. After school he wanted to study in San Francisco, but I couldn't afford it. So he joined the army for a couple of years; he volunteered. And after that he got the money for California together. He joined some big firm while he was still at college. In 2002 he came back to Germany – the firm had problems, I think. Then he started his own company. In Hamburg.'

He drinks a gulp of his beer.

'Aaah.'

'Then what?' I ask.

'Then there was that bank crisis a couple of years ago.'

'2008?'

'Yes, could be; sounds about right. Then my son's firm went bust.'

Swig of beer. Another 'aaah'.

'But he stayed in Hamburg. Works alone now; no firm. For people who call him when they need him.'

'So, a kind of freelance IT consultant?' I ask.

Fuchs shrugs. 'Dunno what that means.'

'When did you last hear from Quirin?' asks Stepanovic, who's been writing everything down.

The old man takes another mighty slug of beer, then he presses the bottle to his heart, looks out of the window and says: 'In the winter.'

NO STARS OVER THE KAISPEICHER A

We've been back up the hill, pinned Fischer down and been shown every corner of the dormitory block: the rooms, whose beds are so unfortunately positioned that, from the doorway, you can't see if the person who sleeps in the corner has been tied to his bunk; the dining room in the cellar; the communal bathrooms where even the ceilings were tiled.

The cold crept into my bones in there, and now I've been freezing for hours, even though it still feels almost like summer.

We're on the motorway again and I can't help staring out of the window the whole time.

We've almost reached Göttingen when Stepanovic asks: 'What are you thinking about?'

'I'd be interested to know what goes on in the heads of adults who think it's right to hand ten-year-olds over to a place like that for five days a week. And I'm wondering who we should be looking for. Schmidt's Cat or Quirin Fuchs?'

'We ought to have the files by the day after tomorrow at the latest. Then we'll have a chance of getting the name of this cat boy. Until then, we concentrate on Quirin Fuchs. Do you want some music on?'

I nod and carry on staring out of the window.

Stepanovic turns the radio on; it's playing a tune that's like a candy cane.

'Yuck, that's sickly,' he says. He fiddles with the tuner and finds some piano concerto or other. 'Ah. Beethoven. Great.'

The music does something to the landscape. Or to me – it's hard to tell the difference. Everything blurs into the notes, outside blends with inside, my blood pulsates and warms, the trees seem to be waving to me, and then to embrace me.

I close my eyes.

And I'm gone.

When I wake up, we're driving under the train tracks south of Hamburg's main station.

'Oops,' I say.

'You're almost home, Riley.'

'How long have we been listening to Beethoven?'

'Forever.'

The music's off again now; there's only the Mercedes, purring steadily away to itself. Stepanovic turns left, into the Speicherstadt.

'Before our trip comes to an end, let's have another smoke.'

He brakes with squealing tyres outside Kaispeicher A. You've been able to park here again since the spring. Last summer, they finally declared the monstrous concert hall built on top of it a failure. After a few months' unbuilding work, there's now a skatepark on the roof. And the little red-and-white ringed lighthouse is back in its old place, a couple of jetties away from the Kehrwiederspitze building. They must have kept it in a safe place somewhere.

'Good spot,' I say.

'The best,' says Stepanovic.

We sit by the lighthouse and smoke. The harbour lights bathe the sky in a dirty orange.

No stars today.

BLACK BOX THREE

My flat seems emptier than usual. I lob my bag into a corner. I feel like company. Question is, whose?

OK: I feel like Faller. I miss him.

I pull out my phone and type a message.

You OK?

Old trick. Ask if everything's OK with the other person, while meaning that something's not really OK with you.

Faller knows that trick.

Yes, just about. How about you?

I miss you.

There's a pause. Then comes a photo. Faller by candlelight on some kind of terrace.

Look at that in the distance. That's the sea.

Hmph.

What are you doing?

I've just got home. I was in Bavaria.

In Bavaria?

The managers in cages, do you remember?

Yes. Hard to forget.

They were at school together, at a boarding school down south. And now we're looking for someone else who was there too. Because, back then, our victims were the bad guys.

And what are they now?

Nothing I'd chat up at the bar.

UNCONSCIOUS ON THE SOFA

'He's gone.'

'Sorry? Hang on, I'll just pop outside.'

I'm standing at the bar in the Blue Night when Stepanovic rings. And because Tuesday is apparently the new going-out day, the place is heaving, and everyone's talking over each other, and the jukebox is bawling that we could be heroes. Whatever. I just had to get out after Stepanovic had dropped me off in my street. And now he's on the line again.

'Who's gone?'

'Sebastian Schmidt.'

'You're kidding me.'

'It's true.'

'Didn't he get a bodyguard?'

'There were two cops outside his door, 24/7,' says Stepanovic. 'They went into the house half an hour ago because neither he nor his wife was responding to calls. It must have only just happened. The French window was open, Schmidt's wife was lying unconscious on the sofa, and Schmidt had disappeared.'

'Quirin Fuchs?' I ask.

'The squad's meeting in ten minutes at Caffamacherreihe.'

'OK,' I say. 'I'm on my way.'

I hang up and go back in to say goodbye to the others. Carla, Rocco and Calabretta are standing at the bar, but they're not standing together. Calabretta is charming a blonde who's rather too tall for him, Carla and Rocco are arguing about something, or at least it looks like they're arguing. Carla has her hands in the air and Rocco's constantly shaking his head.

Klatsche's standing behind the bar, polishing glasses. I try to catch his eye.

I raise my hand.

He doesn't see me.

REVITALISING BATHS

Sahin, Ippig and Acolatse look tired. They've presumably spent the last two days interviewing witnesses nonstop. Sahin marks out on a map of the Altona suburbs where various teams will be searching for traces of Sebastian Schmidt. This produces three concentric circles, spreading out over ever-larger areas. Ippig and Acolatse are sitting at their computers, searching for Quirin Fuchs on the net.

'Got him,' says Acolatse. 'The guy's got a website.'

He puts paper in the printer and here comes the post: the printer spews out an office address, a CV, references, client names and a picture of a thin man with almost shoulder-length dark-blond hair and an angular face.

'OK,' says Stepanovic. 'If he hasn't gone underground, I want him here at a table in the morning. At the moment, he's probably at work on Sebastian Schmidt with God knows what tools.' He shakes himself, almost imperceptibly.

'Who does what?' asks Sahin.

'Riley and I will drive over to see Schmidt's wife in the hospital,' says Stepanovic. 'You and Ippig, coordinate the team looking for Schmidt. Acolatse, grab one of the guys from the station and get Quirin Fuchs here for us. And call me when you've got him, no matter what the time is. I'm not expecting any of us to sleep tonight.'

When he says that, I see the tiredness drain out of their faces. As if everyone has been dipped in a revitalising bath for a second. And been injected with something icy cold.

'We need to get on to the murder squad right away too,' says

Sahin, raising her chin slightly, which immediately makes her look taller. 'After all, Schmidt's their customer for that hit-and-run.'

'True,' says Stepanovic. 'Who'll do that?'

'Me,' I say, 'I will.'

Grab my leather jacket; off I go.

TROUSERS AND HOLSTER

Calabretta answers after the second ring.

'Where are you?' I ask.

'On the sofa,' he says. 'Watching TV. You?'

'Outside the police station on Caffamacherreihe. Hold on tight: Sebastian Schmidt's been kidnapped.'

'You're joking!'

I can literally hear him zap to attention and sit bolt upright on the edge of the sofa.

'Stepanovic and I are about to head over to see his wife, who's in hospital for observation; the rest of the immediate tasks have been delegated. But from first thing tomorrow, we ought all to be working together on the case. Is that OK?'

'You bet that's OK.'

I know he's pleased, and he knows that I'm pleased, even though actually there's nothing pleasing about this. But sometimes it's just the small things. Are men being tortured and stuck in cages every day in your city? Then work on the case with old friends and none of it will be half as bad.

'Where are we working?' he asks, still ready to leap into trousers and holster if I end up saying 'go' after all.

'I'll check tonight,' I say. 'The cage-squad office is too small for eight people. I'll tell you as soon as I know anything. Until then, you can get some sleep.'

'OK,' he says. 'Get stuck in, then.'

I pocket my phone, and I'm pulled up straight, in an old-fashioned way. Like someone who has to walk with a pile of law books balanced on her head. And like I'm very good at it.

THE SADNESS OF THE TISSUE

Angelique Schmidt is not particularly delicate or dainty, but she comes across as a woman that you could snap in the middle with one hand. See-through. As if she's lost an important part of herself a long time ago. She's in the same hospital as Bohnsen and Rösch, and just like those two, she's in a private patient's room with walls painted in friendly colours. Not that that will lessen the shock the evening's caused her. In fact, she's more cowering than lying under her bed-clothes, and she looks at us as though either we or she have come directly from hell. The bedside lamp isn't even trying to produce a cosy atmosphere. The nurse on duty has said that Angelique didn't want a sedative so, as far as she's concerned, we're welcome to go and see her – she probably wouldn't get a wink of sleep all night anyway.

'We only opened the door to the terrace once, briefly,' says Angelique Schmidt. 'Then Sebastian heard something outside and wanted to go and see if next door's dog was running around our garden again.' Her eyes fill with tears. 'I don't know exactly what happened next. I only remember a tall, dark figure coming in through the French window, grabbing me and shoving something into my face.'

'Have you tried calling your husband?' asks Stepanovic.

'His phone is still on the table in the living room,' she says, fumbling with her blanket.

'Were there any phone calls before he disappeared? Did he ring anybody?' asks Stepanovic.

She shakes her head.

'He came home relatively early, about seven. I didn't notice him speaking to anyone on the phone. And he didn't mention it.'

'Can you tell us what your husband was wearing?' I ask.

'Pale chinos, a white shirt. And I think he was wearing his dark-blue boat shoes – he generally does at home.'

Add in hipster glasses and a hipster beard, and we're looking for a man who looks like a hundred thousand other men in this city, especially in Eppendorf and Altona.

She takes a tissue and blows her extremely pointed nose. Stepanovic leans against the window beside her bed.

'Has your husband ever told you about his schooldays?' he asks.

'What do you mean?' She crumples the tissue in her hand. A few question marks float up out of the tissue.

'Well, you know: what the school was like, the stuff he did, the people he spent time with. Stories about teachers, fellow pupils, people from the village. Stuff like that.'

'Hm.' She holds her tissue in her hand. 'I only know that he and Leo and Tobi were there together. And when the two of them were round at ours, they often talked about it. The way you do talk about old times. They laughed a lot then. But I don't know what about. I never really paid much attention.'

'Does the name Quirin Fuchs mean anything to you?'

'No, nothing at all.'

'Ever heard anything about a boy who was known as "the Cat"?'

'No.' She squeezes her hanky. 'Who calls anyone "the Cat"?'

'That's what we're wondering,' says Stepanovic as he lays his card on the bedside table. 'Please call me right away if your husband gets in touch, OK?'

She nods, and now, clearly written across her face, is the great sadness that was buried in the crumpled tissue until a moment ago.

All three of us know that Sebastian Schmidt won't be getting in touch with anybody.

STAY ON THE ROAD

'I'd like to have a look at the Schmidts' house,' says Stepanovic as we climb into his car outside the hospital. 'Right away, ideally. You'll come too, won't you?'

'Is there anyone there to let us in?'

'I'll give them a call.'

He phones. Then he starts the Mercedes. We drive through the darkness. His window is wound halfway down, and for the first time in days, I feel that the air is fresh and cool and clear. The waning moon stands in the sky. That big, battered old thing.

Which? The sky or the moon?

Both, I think.

Every metre we drive along the Elbchaussee, the area gets more expensive and the residents get richer. The properties are lit up on either side of the road – elegant and restrained lighting, yet so skilfully applied that it's impossible to miss the splendour of the gardens and façades. The people who live here are on the winning side. They've been winning since the day they were born. These people have been winning for generations because the rest always lose. Because it's allowed.

Over there, on the left, is a gap between two properties: here, the losers can also get a glimpse of the Elbe. Enjoy the panorama. See the cranes dancing. The lights, the ships, the seabirds. Before the villas are strung together again like pearls on a necklace, and the people made a bit dizzy by seeing such unfamiliar panoramas can creep back into their cellars. Or take the bus.

I don't look.

The Schmidts' house doesn't have a view of the Elbe. It stands on the second row behind the Elbchaussee, in a quiet corner with old, enchanting gardens. A corner for people who don't want to show off quite so demonstrably, or only a little.

'ITK area,' says Stepanovic.

'ITK?'

'In the know. If you know a bit about estate agency, you know that this is the top spot. Costs way more than those hovels down there on the side of the noisy Elbchausee that doesn't even have a river view. But if you're not in the know, you'd think they're just nicely refurbished little houses, not even worth a million.'

He parks the Mercedes on the pavement; we get out and look around.

'But of course they're worth two mill, easily,' he says.

The houses stand a little distance apart from each other, the gardens are planted with roses and hedges and tall trees, the street-lamps give off a muted glow that doesn't shine too piercingly into anybody's bedroom; they even have those extra-soft, yellow light-bulbs screwed into them that they normally only splash out on for photogenic tourist sites.

Perfect for abducting someone from their terrace.

The house is brightly lit. There are police running around both the front and back gardens, forensics are at work, and, here and there, phone calls are being made. A colleague in a white whole-body suit lets us in.

I'd say Scandinavian chic. But the top-end variety. White lime-washed wooden floor, large matt-gold lamps, pale furniture, supposed driftwood on display, painted a mother-of-pearl colour – some pieces have even been made into stands for those ninety-euro scented candles that you can buy in cosmetics shops. It seems that the lady of the house also has a weakness for ikebana and black flower vases. Hanging on the rack in the hall are a pale-grey trench coat, a dark-blue parka with a fur collar, the same thing but in cream, and a red military-style blazer.

'Woah!' says Stepanovic as he walks past.

The hallway has already been turned upside down by our colleagues – there are little markers everywhere with numbers on them. Right now, it's the turn of the terrace, the garden, the living room and the kitchen. They haven't been into the upstairs rooms yet, says the man in the white suit who opened the door to us, so we can't go up there. Basically, we're not allowed to go anywhere except loiter around in the hall, very carefully. But we don't need to. I know what Stepanovic wants. He just wants a look. To have seen the scene of the crime. So that the machine in his head can work better.

'OK,' he says, once he's scanned the living room and the floodlit terrace for maybe ten minutes from the fur-collar-strewn entrance. Then he turns to the investigators in their protective suits who are crawling over the living room floor: 'I presume you're searching every possible escape route for the needle in the haystack.'

'Most definitely.'

We withdraw to let the guys get back to work in peace. We sit in the car, open the doors, and each of us lights a cigarette.

'Do you want to get some sleep or stay up?'

'I don't know,' I say. 'Getting some sleep would probably be more sensible.'

The Mercedes is sitting under a big branch of an apple tree; hanging in front of the windscreen are a couple of apples, almost ripe and already fairly red; they remind me a bit of that special moon the other night.

'Well, I'm not going to get a wink of sleep either way,' he says. 'I'll stay on the road. If you want, I'll drive you home and call you if anything happens.'

He drags on his cigarette. The ember illuminates his profile for a moment, adding a red-light air to the picture. If you judged only by his face, you could take him for a pimp. But lots of policemen look like that.

'Where exactly are you intending to stay out on the road?'

'Would you like to see?'

'Sleep's just a cheap substitute for coffee,' I say.

'You can still ask me to drive you home,' he says, jamming the fag into the corner of his mouth and firing up the engine.

We leave the fancy Elbe suburbs to their fancy fate and drive towards the city centre. On the radio is a somewhat monotonous pop song, but it's fairly well in tune with the feeling of wanting to stay cool and collected, whatever else happens tonight.

And, as we all know, the nights when you've psyched yourself up for something to happen are generally the times when nothing happens at all.

OUT, EVERYBODY OUT OF TIME, NOW

A piano bar in the southern port area; to me, it seems like it's fallen from heaven. An unspectacular, square, single-storey building among all the rusty old industry – but the dark-blue light that falls out of it is a giveaway that something's going on inside. And that something involves music. There are a few cars outside, all relatives of Stepanovic's brown Mercedes. You go in through a steel door and then through a blue bead curtain that hangs right behind the door. There are loads more blue bead curtains, dangling from the ceiling, scattered at random around the room. They sparkle intensely, along with the tiny mirrors in the slowly revolving disco ball, and send blue lights out across the room. In the far-left corner there's a semi-circular bar built into the wall; standing on the bar are a few bottles; there doesn't seem to be a lot of choice. Two sorts of vodka, three sorts of gin, a bit of rum, a bit of brandy, a few bottles of single malt. No beer taps or fridges; all there is beside the glasses, which are piled on a shelf on the wall behind the bar, is a large tub of ice cubes. No bar stools. Left of the bar are three tables, each with three chairs; right of the bar: the same again. That's it for the furniture. Because the room belongs entirely to the somewhat shabby grand piano that stands in the middle. I've never seen a scratched, dusty grand before, a grand that doesn't gleam, a grand that looks like a crow's grandfather. But fine, there's a first time for everything.

Don't know if the piano works. There's nobody playing. The music is coming from two little speakers on the ceiling.

Stepanovic positions himself at the bar and orders a whisky; I position myself next to him and ask for a vodka on the rocks with lemon.

'I had no idea this was here,' I say.

'You ought to stay out and about with me more often,' he says. 'You learn these things.'

Apart from us, there are four other customers here; counting the barman, there are seven of us altogether. All smoking. The barman has a cigarette in his hand while he gets our drinks. He's wearing a black suit, a white shirt and a very thin black tie. And has black hair with lots of pomade.

I keep my eyes fixed on the barman and the bottles of spirits, while Stepanovic looks rather too actively at me from the side. Obviously, that was going to happen at some point. And then there are all these flying lights. It's like a snowstorm in the corner of my eye, and I know that if I look over now, I'll have to say something about it, do something with it, recognise it at least, because it's not hiding away. Stepanovic is imagining something, and he's asking himself questions, and it's possible that he'll ask me some too. But that doesn't suit me at the moment. I want everything to stay the way it is.

I drink my vodka as soon as I've got it standing in front of me, and I order another straight away.

'A double this time, please.'

'There's no rush, Riley. We don't have to leave this place all night if we don't want to.'

'I'm not rushing,' I say, 'I'm just being thorough. This is no place for half measures, is it?'

He takes a sip of his whisky.

'First and foremost, this is an important place. A beautiful slap in the face to all that infrastructure shit at the harbour that doesn't even need people any more. This joint here might be the only place in the whole port that would go under right away without people.'

'How often do you come here?'

'Whenever I can't go home.'

The barman puts my vodka under my nose.

'And why can't you go home when you can't go home?'

'It's your turn to ask questions now, is it?'

He stubs out his cigarette and immediately lights another. And suddenly he looks as though all the colour's been drained out of him, as if a black-and-white comic has accidently left him lying around in the street, and the comic is now running around all over the port because it can hardly bear life without this lost, smoking drawing.

'I can't go home,' he says, 'because I haven't been able to get out of the present for years.'

'What?'

'I can't get out of the present.'

He looks at his hand, the one holding the whisky glass.

'I can't travel through time. I'm a kind of anti-Delorean, if you see what I mean.'

'No,' I say. 'Hang on, I'll have another drink and then maybe I'll get it.'

'It's really not that complicated,' he says. 'Everybody has a connection to time, don't they? You understand what yesterday was, and if you're lucky that means you know why things are the way they are today. Or you think about tomorrow being a new day, and then maybe your mind fills up with the things to do then.'

He sips cautiously at his whisky. I get the general feeling that he's being an awful lot more careful than usual at the moment. The crash-bang Croat seems to have blown away.

'And I can't do that. I just can't access it. Emotionally, I can't linger in either my past or my future. I don't even have the last half-hour or the next ten minutes in my heart. I'm always exactly here and exactly now, without a sense of what brought me here, or what I want to do, or could do, next.'

'How long have you been like that?'

'For a few years. Perhaps I always have been. No idea.'

'And what's so bad about it?'

He drags on his cigarette, and a little bit of the ash falls in my drink. Alas.

'I'm completely at the mercy of every moment,' he says quietly. 'Can you imagine what that's like?'

'Tell me.'

'You come home after a long day. That day, there was a row, violence, a couple of bodies, maybe even a dead child. And then you're standing in an empty flat with a crowded head, and your walls are shouting at you, and nothing in the world can persuade you that this sensation comes from somewhere else; that it's not normal; that it will pass. So you just stand there and you let the moment scream at you and you have no idea if it'll ever stop.'

He takes another sip of whisky.

'I'm like one of those dogs tied up outside the supermarket. Do you know why they always look so sad?'

I shake my head.

'Because dogs have no sense of time. They think everything's forever. They think that they'll have to spend the rest of their lives sitting outside the supermarket.'

'No.'

'Yes.'

I take his half-empty glass and push it over to the barman. He fills it up.

'Why do we always talk about this kind of stuff?' I ask.

'No idea. Doesn't matter anyway.'

'Know what?' I say. 'I'm the exact opposite of you. I can't even get at a moment when I'm in the middle of it. I'm always at a distance from everything.'

He drains the new whisky in one. I'm gradually starting to hope very seriously that nobody will call us tonight. And I think we ought both to get a couple of hours' sleep before we open our mouths again first thing tomorrow. I think that I'll get a taxi soon. And I'll take Stepanovic with me, wherever he wants to go.

'Excuse me,' he says, and as he walks past me, he briefly lays his hand on my shoulder like an old friend. But he only goes two steps, and he doesn't go to the door marked 'WC'; he walks to the middle of the room, he sits down at the piano and starts to play.

At first, I don't recognise the song, because it's kind of a crude jazz version of an old radio tear-jerker. But suddenly I know it. It's 'The End of the World'. The words say something about the world ending when love is lost.

I wonder quite what must have happened to someone for him to have songs like that in his repertoire, and then something dawns on me regarding those moments when his brain is out of time.

I order another two drinks and light two fresh cigarettes. Then I sit down beside him, but unobtrusively.

SHADOWRUNNER

You don't ask questions.

You're the only one who doesn't ask questions.

The other two were both very keen to ask the meaning of this.

You know what this is about without me needing to tell you.

Knowing that stuff makes you the leader.

Being able to smell what's going on.

I take the pliers, apply them and squeeze.

Your eyes widen, they almost pop out of your head, but you don't scream.

Oh yeah, the gag. You can't even scream.

Perhaps that's why you're not asking either.

THEN I WON'T SAY A WORD

Quirin Fuchs has been at police HQ since the early hours. We've left him there, waiting for us, it's what you do. But it couldn't have been helped anyway, because Stepanovic and I were caught in that temporal loop, Cap'n.

Fuchs wears black. Black shirt, black jacket, black trousers. He's enormously tall and well built: almost six foot six, and it feels like he's about three feet wide. A man who does a lot of sport, possibly almost too much – his jacket strains a little uncomfortably over his triceps. His dark-blond hair is combed back and falls below his jaw. He's sitting, leaning back, in one of the interview rooms, his arms crossed over his chest, and he's looking at us as if we were here for a coffee. That's good. It's good when they're not afraid. When you're afraid, you can't think, and we want them to think. And then we want to read the thoughts and extract them.

Stepanovic introduces us both; we sit on the chairs on the other side of the table.

Fuchs smiles at us.

Stepanovic smiles back; me too, but, as far as possible, I keep in the background. Beyond the background, further back.

Calabretta and Anne Stanislawski are standing behind one of the big one-way mirrors on the right-hand wall, listening in.

'Mr Fuchs,' says Stepanovic, 'do you know why you're here?'

'I can imagine.'

Deep voice, soft tone; you could sell it directly to the radio.

'Well then, that's a good start for a constructive conversation, don't you agree?'

Fuchs nods, still smiling.

'Then would you please tell us why you think we'd like to speak to you?'

'I suspect that you'd like to speak to me about violence,' he says, sitting up straight and laying his hands on the table. 'But I don't want to talk about violence right now. We might get on to violence later. I'd like to speak to you about justice.'

He undoubtedly takes the point for best opening.

'Whew,' says Stepanovic, scratching his head. 'That's a little on the large side to start off with. Why don't we begin by clearing up a few facts?'

Fuchs looks at us impassively. Waits. His eyes say: come on, then.

'For instance, we'd simply love to know where Sebastian Schmidt is,' says Stepanovic. 'And we're hoping that you can help us with that.'

Fuchs leans a forwards little and says: 'I can. But I'll do you a deal.'

'A deal?'

I don't know Stepanovic particularly well, but I'm pretty sure he's not the type who goes in for deals.

'You invite Yannick Katsarou to our conversation,' says Fuchs, 'and in return I'll tell you everything I know.'

'Who's Yannick Katsarou?' asks Stepanovic, and everything about him that just now seemed friendly and approachable has turned edgy and hard. That may also be because we've had Quirin Fuchs sitting in front of us for less than ten minutes, and already the reins are slackening on us. This wasn't actually the plan.

'A journalist,' I say and I'm extremely glad that I happen to know that right at this moment. 'I've just been reading something about him. He runs that economics blog; what's its name again?'

'Economi.co,' says Fuchs. 'Exciting project, in my opinion. Katsarou is an impressive young man, doesn't mince his words.'

'Some journalists accuse him of left-wing populism,' I say. 'Or so I've heard.'

Man. Look what happens when I read the paper.

Stepanovic gestures soothingly.

'I really don't care who accuses him of what. I categorically refuse to bring a journalist in on an investigation in progress.'

Quirin Fuchs leans back again.

'Then I won't say a word. You decide which you prefer.'

Stepanovic stands up – rather too abruptly to pass for even remotely unfazed – and looks at me.

'Coffee?'

I think I should nod. I nod.

'Good,' he says. 'Let's both go and get a cup.'

He leaves the windowless room without asking Fuchs if he'd also like a coffee, which is all part of the game. Fuchs grasps that immediately but, in contrast to us, he doesn't let it unsettle him, and he keeps smiling quietly away to himself. I don't interfere. I stand up and follow Stepanovic.

The door to the interview room has barely closed behind us when Stepanovic pulls me to him by the sleeve and whispers: 'He wants press?'

'Clearly.'

'And why that guy of all people, that Ka—. What's his name?'

'Katsarou,' I say. 'Well, if you tell a respectable news journalist something, there's a relatively good chance that they'll interrupt to ask awkward questions. But with a blogger, you can recite your message straight into their microphone – they're not beholden to anyone but themselves.'

Stepanovic rubs his temples.

'What d'you make of him?'

'Fuchs?' I ask.

He nods.

'Lucid, shrewd, calm. And pretty determined. At least at first glance.'

Stepanovic topples back against the concrete wall and blows air up towards the ceiling.

Then he straightens up.

'I've cracked everyone so far. He can sod off with his "I want press or I'm not talking to you". We'll see about that.'

We get coffee, look in on Calabretta and Stanislawski and tell them that Fuchs can kiss our arses. And then we go back in.

TURNING POINT

Five hours. Five whole hours we've been sitting here now, facing each other, and Quirin Fuchs hasn't uttered a sound. He's still sitting silently and smiling.

Stepanovic, on the other hand, is giving it his all. He talks and eases the situation. He lays photos of Rösch and Bohnsen in front of Fuchs, tortured and untortured, and tortured again. He tells him that we've spoken to his father. He tells him how his father's getting on. He stands up and goes out and takes me with him. He goes back in and puts coffee on the table. He swaps the team around: sometimes me, sometimes him; and then, instead of me or him, there's Calabretta or Anne Stanislawski around the table; and then it's back to us two again. He offers time, understanding and threats. He offers cigarettes and more coffee and redemption. Deluxe model interrogation technique. I can hardly bear it, and I could swear that the pale-grey walls are slowly closing in on us. The room grows smaller with every passing hour.

But Fuchs smiles silently.

'OK,' says Stepanovic, 'OK. What's the point of the thing with this journalist? Explain it to me, and I'll think about it.'

Fuchs takes a deep breath. He knows that at that second, the game has turned.

'I've got nothing left to lose,' he says. 'And I want everyone to understand why. Because – now, pay attention – there's massive shit happening out there. That shit's been happening for ages and it's still going on, and I want it finally stopped. You get Katsarou in this room, give him permission to listen, record and ultimately publish my story exclusively, and your case will be closed in two days. Success. I give you my word.'

He stands up and holds out his hand to Stepanovic.

'And success is what we all want, isn't it?'

'Sit down, please,' says Stepanovic.

Stepanovic apparently no longer wants to discuss things outside; instead, he just turns briefly to me and says: 'So, as far as I'm concerned, this hack can sit in. What does the prosecution have to say?'

'If it helps to get at the truth,' says the Prosecution Service.

'It will,' says Quirin Fuchs. 'Promise.'

I stand up, and go out and talk to Calabretta. He says Yannick Katsarou will be rounded up and brought over here ASAP. If he's even half as keen on exclusives as I suspect, he'll be at the door in half an hour.

WE WEREN'T LIVING, WE WERE JUST WAITING FOR IT TO BE OVER

We meet Yannick Katsarou at the lift. A slightly chubby guy in his late twenties with fuzzy curls. He's wearing jeans, a grey college jacket and a shirt printed with Mos Eisley Cantina band tour dates. He's also airing a cheeky and ultra-self-confident grin.

'Why does he want me of all people?' he asks, even before we've said hello.

'I think he likes your style,' I say and hold out my hand. 'This is an absolute exception, got that? Not a word about it to anyone.'

He, somewhat touchingly, clicks the heels of his trainers together.

'I get my story, you get your statement, or else nobody gets anything.' He looks me in the eye. 'And if not, you'll rip me to shreds.'

'Why should I?' I ask, and I think: just like your serious colleagues will rip me to shreds if they get wind of what's happened here. I'll be lucky if I still have a job next week.

Then the three of us head for the interview room.

Stepanovic's discomfort is so obvious that I'd like to call a beer lorry for him right away.

As we walk in and Quirin Fuchs sees the young journalist, something settles over his face. A kind of soft-focus filter. As if he hadn't realised how badly he'd missed someone until they'd come into the room. I reckon Fuchs was maybe a bit less certain that his little game would work than we thought he was.

'Good,' he says, more to himself than to us, once he's greeted Yannick Katsarou and sat down again. 'Very good.'

Katsarou takes the chair that's standing by the table next to Fuchs and drags it round to the side. Stepanovic and I sit back down in the two seats opposite Quirin Fuchs.

'Your journalist, sir,' says Stepanovic, looking at Fuchs and pointing at Katsarou. 'Now, get going.'

'Wait a minute,' says Katsarou as he lays his phone on the table. 'Can I record this, or do I get that there?' He points at the voice recorder standing in the middle of the table.

'Neither,' I say. 'But you may take notes. And our questions are not to feature. Only the statements made by Mr Fuchs.'

He looks wide-eyed at me. Fuchs too. Now we're setting the terms again. The other two exchange a long look. Fuchs' expression is almost pleading; Katsarou's starts off completely blank, but then: well, then.

I don't like the boy and I say: 'Pad? Pen?'

'Yeah, got 'em.'

'Then grab them quickly, I think we're about to start.'

Something about this guy is seriously winding me up. Keep calm. And leave the rest to Mr Stepanovic.

He switches on the recorder. Katsarou has actually managed to fish a pad and pen out of his shoulder bag.

'Mr Fuchs,' says Stepanovic, 'where is Sebastian Schmidt?'

Fuchs shakes his head.

'No. No, no, no. We'll start elsewhere. And if you listen to me carefully, I'll tell you where you can find Sebastian at the end.'

Stepanovic inhales audibly, and exhales.

'OK. So where are we starting from?'

'You said earlier that you went to see my dad.'

'Yes.'

'Did you go to the school too?'

'We did.'

'How did you like Biesendorf?'

'You were going to talk, not us.'

'True.'

He pushes the chair back a little way, crosses his long legs and briefly reassures himself that Katsarou really is writing this down. His pen's at the ready. OK.

'I never dreamt it would work that well. That any of you would get the idea of looking into that crappy boarding school. You can't imagine what it was like. Nobody can imagine, and if they can, nobody wants to believe it. Matt and me, we weren't living in Biesendorf – we were just waiting for it to be over.'

'What was this Matt's surname?' asks Stepanovic.

'Can't remember.'

They're Buying Themselves Islands in the North Atlantic, but That Won't Protect Them
(Exclusively from us to you)
Transcript: Yannick Katsarou

I was a quiet child who often played alone. Mostly, I sat down by the stream and talked to the frogs. Or I built secret machines out of the broken tools that my father kept leaving outside his workshop in the yard. Generally speaking, I avoided people's attention. My parents rarely had to tell me off and I did well at school right from the start. I didn't bother anyone, which people in a Bavarian village tend to like in a child. When it became clear that I'd get into grammar school, that obviously meant the school on the hill, the boarding school. That was where all the village grammar school kids went. The others were allowed to go to the high school in the next town. I would have preferred to go there too because the three other boys in my primary school class were going there and I thought they were my friends. But when they found out that I was going to the grammar school, they beat me up in the bushes behind the old mill. Then they never spoke to me again.

On my first day at the grammar school, nobody spoke to me either, because I was the only dumpster – a day kid, a village kid; not a boarder, you know? Dumpsters were immediately at the bottom of the heap right as far as the boarders were concerned; as a dumpster you were the lowest of the low. I didn't understand all that, but I didn't stick up for myself either because I wouldn't have known how. My parents, my uncle and aunts, our neighbours from the village – they wouldn't have known how either. We weren't the sort to stick up for ourselves. We were people who didn't bother anyone.

So I spent the afternoons either playing alone again, or sitting in my room with a maths book on my knees. I was really good at maths, even better than I was at all the other subjects, but at school I tried not to show it.

After six months, Matthias joined our class. He was nice. A bit smaller and thinner than the rest of us. He said we could call him Matt. But nobody cared what they could call the new boy, because he was just the new boy. He came from a small town north of Würzburg and had been sent to the boarding school by children's services, not by his parents. He never told me what was up with his parents, but there was something; at any rate he never went home for the weekend. Weekends were the good days for us, because apart from us and a few others with problems at home, there was nobody there. Then we spent all day playing Shadowrun, either in my room or, in nice weather, on the old garden table behind the house. As a Shadowrunner, you were an agent, hired by big multinational companies, and you had to get information that your company could use to ruin the other companies. Or bump the other agents off right away. We sat there like that with a game that consisted of a couple of dice and a set of rules and, in our heads, we were awesome. Highly intelligent, dangerous spies. We played in the week too, on a corner table in the common room, because in the week, pupils weren't allowed far from the school and my parents' house was outside the permitted range.

But weekdays were bad days for us.

Because, in the week, Matt wasn't Matt but Schmidt's Cat. He'd been put in a room with Sebastian, Leonhard and Tobias. Perhaps Matty would have fared badly in any room, being the way he was, and looking the way he did, with his nerdy glasses. But I reckon that room was the worst of all. Because those three were the worst of all. And because they'd got the teachers under their thumbs. The three of them had absolutely nothing to fear. And they treated Matty like he wasn't human.

He never wanted to talk about it, but every morning I could see what they'd done overnight. Bad stuff. And the older they got the worse the stuff got. At first, they just held his fingers in warm water while he was asleep to make him wet the bed, or simply shoved him under the cold shower. Later, they got really brutal. Then there were burns on his arms and on his face. And there were days when he couldn't sit down because they'd given him such a good seeing to at night, all three of them. At least he told me about that – just once. And from then on, I dreamt almost every night of killing those wankers. What Matty dreamt about, I don't know. Nothing at all, maybe.

The teachers and school management looked away. I remember at some point writing letters. To Sebastian's and Leo's and Tobi's parents. I even wrote to children's services and the education authorities. Nobody responded.

And then, when we were fifteen, I went into class one morning and Matt wasn't there. There were rumours: he'd had a seizure. Epilepsy. Or he'd got a really high fever. Or a dangerous vomiting bug.

But I know what happened, I know what he did. Some of us were already shaving. Matt had collected the discarded razor blades from the bins in the bathroom and he'd saved the best ones, the ones that were still sharp. For a while I thought he was doing that so that he could defend himself against them. But that morning, I knew what he'd had in mind. I didn't speak a word about it to anyone in that school until I'd finished my exams, and then I went to study in San Francisco.

And?

That's enough of a reason, isn't it?

Isn't that enough reason to collar the three of them at night, in the underground car park or on their fancy terraces, and shove chloroform in their faces and hurt them a bit? To show them to people as they are? Sordid, scratched, like predators that you have to shut up in a cage? Easily enough, in my opinion.

But those guys went one better.

They didn't just get away with what they did to Matty for years and years; they carried on getting worse, year after year, just as they did back then. Except that now they wear suits and they've learnt to behave if anyone's watching.

They sit there in their deluxe executive chairs, earning sacks of money while other people lose their jobs. They're part of the group that cements this social order in which more and more people are afraid, and fewer and fewer can feel secure. And it doesn't bother them.

They're not remotely bothered that every time they fire someone for financial reasons, it creates a vote that the fascists celebrate as a success – because fear makes people stupid. And why aren't they bothered? Simple: because they're fascists themselves. Money fascists. Anybody who doesn't help to earn them more money has to go, has no rights. Anyone who helps them consolidate their power gets fucked.

So that really would be enough reason, wouldn't it? That would easily be enough reason to lock the three of them in cages, to put them on display, to point the finger at them and say to people: look at what's destroying you. Arseholes like this are destroying you.

It would have been enough, obviously; everyone would have understood, wouldn't they? Everyone.

But they still went one better.

One just for me.

When I came back from Silicon Valley to Germany in the early noughties, I founded a start-up here in Hamburg. We used our expertise and technology to help magazines and newspapers get online and where possible to earn more money. It wasn't going terribly well, because none of the publishers wanted to spend much money on it; they didn't think online media were important enough. But it was going well enough for my few guys and me to survive; there were just enough new magazines who caught on early to what it was all about – the future. And one day, I had a stroke of genius. A kind of daily bundle of texts from the print media that customers could subscribe to. You got an email offering articles that weren't freely available on the web, and you could buy them individually for a tiny sum and read them as a PDF. Then, at the end of the month, a few euros would be taken off your credit card. All very easy, all very modern.

To this day, I don't know what got into me, what made me go to Mohn & Wolff. I knew who the management team were. Perhaps I thought that, if I presented them with this idea, they'd finally realise who I really was, who they'd been underestimating for years. Perhaps I thought now I'd be calling the shots, have the whip hand. If I could wave something they really wanted under their noses. Something they'd really have to shell out for if they wanted it.

Perhaps that's what I thought.

Of course they wanted it. I had a firm agreement, a deadline to deliver the concept and the programme, and I was to take on some staff. Half the money would come on signing the contract and the other half on delivery of our work.

I was so stupid. I believed them.

Rented a new office. Hired people. Bought bigger computers. Worked round the clock.

Just before the contract was due to be signed, I got a call from Sebastian. Mohn & Wolff had changed its mind. They'd realised that the idea had no future. Sadly, the deal was off. But I should feel free to contact them if I came up with anything else.

He wished me the best of luck with my deliberations.

I lost everything. I couldn't pay the rent on the new office. I sold the new computers at a loss. Of course, the staff had notice periods that I had to keep to. I went bankrupt.

Since then, I've been paying off my debts, working as a poorly paid, freelance IT consultant. Nobody will give me a job at any of the major German publishers, not even freelance, and I refuse to believe that that's a coincidence.

Now that really and truly would be enough to seriously hurt my three former schoolmates. It's enough to make anyone lose their rag; anybody would be able to relate to that, wouldn't they?

First, they spend years torturing my only friend, then they wallow in success, and they end up humiliating and ruining me – is anyone surprised that I'm furious?

But for Sebastian, Leo and Tobi, even that wasn't enough. They wanted to see me even more down and out, even if it was only in their imaginations. For about the last six months, they've been accepting praise for a new idea. Not just at Mohn & Wolff but from the whole industry.

It's genius. Listen: a kind of daily bundle of texts from the print media that customers can subscribe to. You get an email offering articles that aren't available on the web and you can buy them individually for a tiny sum and read them as a PDF. Credit card bill at the end of the month. Ultra-cool, ultra-modern.

There was a big article in a trade journal recently, saying that these three men have got where they are today – at the top of Germany's most important magazine publisher – with good reason. Because they've just got a bloody good feeling for when an idea is ripe and ready to conquer the market.

It's always the same arseholes who win.

And nobody punishes them for the fact that they only win because others lose.

Quite the reverse. They get richer and richer, and more and more influential. And everyone makes a massive song and dance about them. Holds doors open for them into shops where you can't buy a pair of underpants for less than a hundred euros. And that makes them feel not just rich but also important. So of course, then they act like they're important. And everyone else makes even more of a song and dance. It's horribly embarrassing. Someone ought to whack them round the head with it the moment they start up. But they know that nobody will whack them round the head, so they don't need to worry. They've learnt that they'll get away with it.

But a couple of them are slowly starting to get scared. They're starting to realise that the world won't put up with their dealings much longer. That maybe people like me will come along more and more often to punish them. Some of them – or so I've heard from my former colleagues in Silicon Valley – have had their eyes lasered, just so they don't have to rely on glasses or contact lenses if things get tricky. They're taking archery lessons. They're stockpiling weapons and ammunition. They're laying in food supplies, filling tanks of drinking water, keeping helicopters ready for take-off on the roof. They're buying land in New Zealand or on islands in the North Atlantic. And if the system they've created breaks down – because they've ruthlessly exploited everything: natural resources, water, people; because they've put whole nations at the service of their system and then made them the losers in it – that's where they'll hide from the rampaging mobs. But nothing will be able to protect them when the wrath of the losers explodes. The wrath will be too much.

In the end, all I've done is to prepare the world for that a bit.

And now you can arrest me.

SOMETHING THAT COULD TIP OVER AT ANY MOMENT

'So, Mr Fuchs,' says Stepanovic. It's just before midnight. In the room, there's a blend of leaden weariness and electrifying tension. 'Where is Sebastian Schmidt? If we find him alive, there can be a relatively easy way out of this for you.'

'You should understand by now that I really don't care whether or not there's an easy way out,' he says. 'I've got nothing left to lose. So as far as that goes, I don't give a shit whether you find Sebastian alive or not. The bigger question is whether he even wants to live.'

'You mean he'd rather die? Because of your campaign? Because of the press? I think you're misjudging him.'

'Not because of me. Because of the girl.'

'What girl?' asks Stepanovic.

'The one he mowed down a few nights back,' says Fuchs.

I look him in the eye and ask: 'How do you know about that?'

'I have my sources.'

He stands up and walks the few steps to the wall, stretches. What's he talking about? What the hell does he mean 'sources'? Who tipped him off? My brain races. I always jump straight to moles in the police, but you can really trust Calabretta's guys.

Mohn & Wolff.

It must have leaked out from there. He must know someone there. And that person can't have wanted Schmidt's hit-and-run to be hushed up. Well. You can't ban people from gossiping about their bosses.

Quirin Fuchs sits down again.

'Another thing,' says Stepanovic. 'Did you ever hear from your friend Matt again?'

'No. I had a very strong feeling back then that he died in hospital.'

And I get a very strong feeling now that, while Fuchs has told us a whole heap of truth, this is a lie. Everything he's said until now has sprung from the deepest conviction. From the inflamed brain of a man with a rock-solid conviction that the world – intentionally – wishes him nothing but ill; of a man who interprets everything that happens in this light: first they destroyed Matt, then they destroyed Mohn & Wolff, then they destroyed me. And anyone who claims otherwise is a liar.

That was how he spat it out. As if he'd been telling himself the same story again and again for years.

The idea that his friend Matt is dead came along very differently, though. Quiet, matter-of-fact, learnt by rote. As if Matty would only die if you spoke it out loud. I suspect we're going to have to check on Matty.

'Why, do you think,' I ask, 'did all these things happen?'

He takes his chair, pulls it round beside me, sits very close and looks at me. Out of the corner of my eye, I can see Stepanovic's neck muscles tensing. I lay a hand on his forearm. It's OK. Quirin Fuchs won't hurt me. I know he's not one of the good guys, but he's not one of the bad guys either.

'I've thought a lot about that,' he says, 'again and again, whole nights long. I think it's like this: everyone wants to mean something to someone. If someone doesn't feel that – doesn't have this sense of a meaning to his life – he starts doing bad things. Or enduring them. Depending on personality.'

'How do you mean?' I ask.

He looks me in the eye with an expression that makes me feel as though I'm getting into a lift down to a dark cellar.

'You know exactly what I mean.'

He knows that I know that he isn't the righteous knight he'd like to market himself as. He knows that I know Matt isn't dead. And he knows that I know what it smells like in those dark cellars, in which we all sit far too often. I could nail him down on that now. On Matty and on an honest conversation, now and here, in this moment, in this cellar. But I'd rather not. I'd rather get out of the cellar again please.

Stepanovic stands up.

'So. Now you'll take us to Sebastian Schmidt.'

Fuchs shuts his eyes and takes a deep breath.

'Right you are. Let's go.'

As if he's left something behind for me that could tip over at any moment.

A BARE LIGHTBULB, DANGLING FROM THE CEILING

I can never remember the real name of this street – I always call it Hardcorestrasse. Because it's such a hard break. One minute, cuddly Altona, then you turn right by mistake and suddenly you're bang in the middle of post-industrial malaise. Factories and workshops standing empty, lots of red brick, lots of barred windows, here and there a building that may be a house but is certainly not a home, then an expensive restaurant or a snotty bar suddenly pops up in between them, right next door to another kiosk that has a couple of very pasty, or very haggard, figures clinging to it because it mainly sells alcohol, and sometimes sweets, but only in secret.

We're all travelling together. Stepanovic, Sahin, Ippig and me in one car; Calabretta and Anne Stanislawski driving directly behind us; up ahead is the police car with Quirin Fuchs on the back seat. Schulle, Brückner and Acolatse are holding the fort at HQ.

The patrol car turns off to the left and drives into a gravelled courtyard. The grey building on the left-hand side looks like a warehouse; the windows are smashed and there are a couple of rusty vans in front of it, though they don't look exactly roadworthy. The brick building on the right could once have been a brickworks or something like that; at any rate it's got an impressive chimney that proclaims, clearly and unmistakably, that this is a place where, over the decades, many things have been subjected to intense heat.

The police car drives once around the building, all our cars following behind; we stop in front of the rear entrance and get out. Quirin Fuchs leads the way, flanked by two uniformed police officers. He opens the back door, which is obviously unlocked. There's no light.

'You must have torches with you,' he says to the policemen.

They have. And they switch them on.

We follow Fuchs down a dark corridor. Then down some stairs. Through a door that's slightly ajar. Fuchs presses a light switch on the wall; a bare lightbulb, dangling from the ceiling, comes on.

'There's nobody here,' says one of the policemen.

'No,' says Fuchs.

We all stand there, gawping like a load of goldfish.

CHANCE BLOWN

'He was here,' says Fuchs, leaning against the dirty, blood-stained bunk, from which dangle four loose leather belt-ends; the buckles have been cut off and are lying on the floor. 'I fetched him from his terrace. I had him here in the cellar. Then I went home. Your colleagues were waiting for me there, and they took me with them.'

'All the doors we just came through were open,' says Stepanovic. 'Who else knows their way around here? Who has a key?'

'I only have the key to this room here,' says Fuchs, as he reaches into his trouser pocket and holds up an unspectacular house key. 'I have no idea who else might have one. But I didn't lock up when I left.'

'Why not?' I ask.

'Hey, I'm not imprisoning anyone here.'

He looks at me, and only me, and he gives a sly grin. And this moment is the first time that he strikes me as properly unlikeable.

'Where did you get the key from?' I ask.

'Found it.'

Until a couple of minutes ago, I was actually toying with the idea of maybe losing track of him on his journey into custody – losing him, letting him get lost, whatever. But now I feel taken for a ride. Now rage is rising up within me. I can be OK with someone avenging an old friend, but I'm very much not OK with it if he's only thinking of himself while he does. And I wonder why he didn't help his old friend at the time. He's tall, he's strong, even as an adolescent he won't have been a bantamweight. Why didn't he stand up for his friend thirty years ago? Why did he leave him to these three arseholes and their nasty tricks without tackling them? Because he wasn't angry enough until they did something to him too. He's an egotistical coward who only feels good if he can blame other people for the way his life's turned out. And who, decades after the event, has finally seen an opportunity to rub those others' noses in their guilt.

I'd have been prepared to forgive him for that. I'd have been prepared to take his side because I like to be on the side of the angry. But, sadly, he just blew the chance to draw me in. With a single sly grin.

'Who knew that Sebastian Schmidt was here, Mr Fuchs?'

This is Calabretta, and I get the impression that he's pretty angry too. He can't stand anyone pinching a suspect off him.

Quirin Fuchs lies on the bed, links his arms behind his head and closes his eyes. I know the expression on his face.

He won't utter another word.

'Take him away,' I say.

TOGETHER, NOT GOING HOME

We've handed the cellar over to SOCO, and Quirin Fuchs has been remanded in custody. Now we're standing around on the street outside, smoking. Calabretta, Anne Stanislawski, Stepanovic and me. Sahin and Ippig have gone home – they wanted to grab a bit of sleep, which is obviously extremely sensible.

Calabretta looks around the circle and says: 'Well, I'd imagine that Sebastian Schmidt's just legged it, given that all the doors were open. Who knows how tightly Fuchs left him tied up…'

'I can't shake that idea, either,' says Stepanovic. 'It'd be a good opportunity for him, wouldn't it? A chance to disappear. After all, he's got a hit-and-run and a dead girl hanging round his neck.'

Anne Stanislawski wrinkles her nose and then her forehead.

'How could he vanish without help? Even if he got out of here alone, even if Fuchs – for whatever reason – made it possible, factored it in. Schmidt started out lying on the sofa at home. He didn't even have his phone on him, let alone a credit card or anything. And he can't go home if he's planning to disappear. After all, we're there, or our colleagues are.'

Her eyes follow my cigarette.

'That's how I see it too,' I say. 'Either he's about to cast himself, whimpering, into the arms of the police at home, or someone got him out of there.'

The two men growl.

Stepanovic looks at his watch; you can just make out the dial in the streetlights. It's almost half past one.

'Guys,' says Anne Stanislawski, rubbing her right eye, 'I need some kip. See you first thing tomorrow, yeah?'

'Right you are, Anne,' says Calabretta. 'I'll drive you home. I've got plans, but you're more or less on the way.'

Since when has everyone been on first-name terms with each other?

And Calabretta has plans?

Nuts.

We murmur good-night pleasantries and there are high fives here and there, and then Ivo Stepanovic and I are alone again.

He chucks his dog-end away and shoves his hands in his trouser pockets and for a moment he looks like a teenager.

'So? Shall we not go home together?'

'When do you actually sleep?' I ask.

'In between times. How about you?'

'In passing.'

'Well then,' he says, taking his left hand out of his trouser pocket and putting an arm round my waist. 'Let's get out of here.'

'Oi. Hands off.'

'Sorry.'

He lets go, walks to the passenger side of the Mercedes and opens the door for me.

'After you, ma'am. The special service to Not Going Home will depart in two minutes.'

'You showed me yours,' I say as I get in. 'Now I'll show you mine.'

He looks at me as if I were a patient and he were the operating surgeon.

'I can hardly wait.'

SACK OF CEMENT

'Hans-Albers-Platz? Are you nuts, Riley?'

'It gets better.'

We fight our way through heaps of drunks and shards of glass, we don't let the pop music creep into our ears, we cling only to each other's presence. There, on the far left, shines the Blue Night. It might be daft to turn up at Klatsche's with Stepanovic. It could go completely wrong, but I feel like it, and I just want to see what happens.

Perhaps everything will resolve into something all of a sudden.

Ha ha.

I stand in the doorway. The candles are lit; the red neon script over the bar fills the room with the pub's name. There are people sitting and laughing at the tables, a couple standing by the bar, one or two not actually laughing; a young woman is leaning against the jukebox, crying into her long drink. Behind the bar is Rocco, opening beer bottles. Guitar music gurgles from the speakers.

'Nice place,' says Stepanovic. He stands beside me and looks round.

'Yes,' I say, 'but there's something missing.'

I walk over to Rocco and say: 'Hello, Hamburg Public Prosecution Service.'

'Hey,' he says quietly and smiles. The smile is one of the feigned sort and hurts, although I'm sure it hurts him more than it does me.

'Where's Klatsche?' I ask.

He shrugs.

'Out. He left two hours ago, didn't say where he was going.'

'And Carla?'

'How would I know?'

He looks over to the door, where Stepanovic is still standing. Plain-clothes cop, you can smell it from ten miles upwind.

'Colleague of yours?'

I nod.

'Shall I open you a couple of beers?'

'Leave it,' I say, 'I was heading home.'

'OK,' he says.

I say nothing because there's a lump in my throat. It's awful leaving him here like this, but sometimes things are just awful.

At the door I thump Stepanovic in the side and say: 'Come on.'

'I thought you wanted to show me your not-home.'

'I'll show you another. Do you know the Sorgenbrecher?'

'Worry-Breaker? Perfect name for everything.'

He offers me his arm. I link up. After all, you need some way of clambering safely over all these heaps of glass, sad people and bad music.

At the Sorgenbrecher, I unlink again because, all in all, there's a much surer footing in there.

'Watch out, though,' I say as we walk through the door, 'they mix them strong here.'

'So I see,' says Stepanovic, looking over to the little bench in the far corner.

There's Calabretta.

He's mid-snog.

With a very exciting woman.

She has her legs crossed and she's wearing black high-heeled shoes, a short black skirt and a tight black shirt. Her long dark curls are falling right across her face. I try to swallow down the thought that this woman bears an uncanny resemblance to … But, just at that moment, Calabretta strokes back her hair and I can't hide away from it any longer: the woman is Carla.

'Er,' I say.

'Bit of a lady's man, our colleague, eh? Come on, let's not disturb them.'

Stepanovic takes me by the hand and pulls me outside. I can't move properly; it must feel like dragging a sack of cement over rough wood.

The only thing that works here is the door.

Once it's shut behind us, there's a very unpleasant sound in my head. As if something might explode in there any moment.

'Where now?' he asks.

'Nowhere,' I say. And turn around and run off.

THEN CRASH, HARD

Calabretta.

He must have pretty broad shoulders right now. Got over the shock of Betty dumping him and the lovelorn-misery thing; is investigating a spectacular hit-and-run; and the Albanian, his old enemy, is six feet under, shot in the head. So then, of course, why wouldn't you say: sod it. Who cares if it all goes tits up? All that shit. And why wouldn't you fool about at the very centre of your circle of friends. Regardless of the consequences. If you're the main man, you can do that.

Bloody hell.

How about you?

What do you see?

When you look at me, for example?

I don't even know how long you've been watching me. A couple of years, maybe. Maybe a couple of hours. I'd really love to know what you see, what else there is for you to see apart from the rather comic-book face, the overlarge lips, the slightly crooked nose and the tired eyes, which always come across as too heavily made up, but that's just the dark circles because I don't wear any make-up. What do you see, apart from the tall, slightly bony body and the long reddish-brown hair that almost always looks straight out of a shampoo ad? Sometimes I'm genuinely embarrassed by the way people secretly stare at it. I can't help my hair being the way it is. At least it's starting to go grey.

What do you see when you look me in the eyes?

When we stand facing each other? When I look at you, late at night, with a few neon signs around my head; with the now flawlessly renovated art nouveau façades behind me, lining my path to left and right? Or, when you gaze at this vista, those same façades forming the backdrop to my life and to the deaths of the others? Blurred in the background are a few windows where there are still lights on, or at least a TV.

And can you hear my boots clatter? The sound of my boots at night is part of me, an important part. At night, on the streets, I'm safe; the city streets at night are my home. I'm not lonely here, and nobody is superfluous. Clack, clack. Clack, clack. At night, on the streets, I can think without having to run away from anything. At night, on the streets, it's never far to the nearest bar.

I think: what's going on here? Why am I responsible? Why do they let me off the leash for their 'special assignments'? And will I soon, when we've broken up the cage squad, be sitting back in my witness-protection room? When will they let me out next? Maybe never? They can't chuck me out altogether. They're afraid that I might talk. About what happened at the harbour that time, when I shot that guy's balls off. They're afraid I might tell someone that, after the shooting, absolutely nothing happened that should have. Disciplinary procedures, outcry in the press about arbitrary force from the Public Prosecution Service, witch hunt. They're afraid I might say the guy was just gone, and so was my dad's army pistol, and that was that. That I was protected as well as side-lined. That I don't talk too much about what I found out about my boss.

This much is clear: if they want to get rid of me, they'll have to kill me.

How would you decide?

I'd let them kill me. Then I'd finally be free of this feeling I get as soon as I get outside: just don't mess up or you'll be sitting back in your box, and forever this time.

Maybe I should talk to the attorney general, Dr Kolb. But maybe better not.

Sometimes I think we trust each other. And then I think: not as far as I can throw you, lady.

Excuse me, you don't happen to know where Klatsche is, do you? And what's actually wrong with me and him? Is it just a matter of time? Before … whatever?

Bugger that; I don't want to know.

Would you want to know?

Don't tell me right now.

And you needn't comment on Stepanovic either. It is what it is, even if I don't know whether I like it. We'll see. You know how it is: keep riding the punk train from one night to the next. Don't get stopped. Then crash, hard.

Now look there. Over there is the edge of the port; there the cranes are towering into the sky. Once you get there, with a view of the docks, everything comes to a standstill and, further out, things carry on, but differently.

Maybe I should have let Fuchs go? Didn't he deserve to get away?

Turn left, down this beer trail.

The flashing red neon heart

of the Maria Bar

blinks me over the brink

BLACK BOX FOUR

My telephone rings. It's Spain.

'Hey, Faller.'

'Where are you?'

'At home.'

'Why's that?'

'It's almost three.'

'Oh, right.'

'Faller?'

'Yes?'

'What's up?'

'I'm flying back tomorrow and just wanted to talk to you.'

'Now it's autumn, you're coming back?'

'Can't deal with the good weather any longer. It depresses me.'

'Well you'll like it here. It's just starting to rain.'

'Really?'

'Yes.'

I open the window and hold the phone up to the rain. It set in a couple of minutes ago, and at this very moment it turns into a cloudburst. As if it hasn't rained for years, as if the sky was just way too full of everything.

'Wow. Hamburg.'

'All the same as ever.'

'How's everything else?'

'We've got a culprit. And he's also a victim.'

'So that's just the same as ever too, isn't it?'

'The same as most of the time. The interesting thing is that the guy whose turn it was to be found in a cage next has disappeared.'

'Doesn't seem to bother you particularly.'

'He's an arse. It looks very much as though he ran a young woman over and just left her there. That really nasty hit-and-run. If I'm honest, I don't give a damn about him.'

At the other end of the line, a cigarette is lit. Here too.

'How long's he been gone?'

'A day or two, depending how you look at it.'

'Meaning?'

'Too complicated.'

'Well, then, I can't wait to see if he's returned by tomorrow, when I'm back.'

'That'd be a thing, Faller.'

'If not, you can forget it anyway.'

'What do you mean?'

'Don't you know the old rule of thumb? If you're looking for someone and you haven't got them after forty-eight hours, the chances of catching them are piss poor.'

'I didn't know that.'

'It's particularly true of fugitives and anyone who wants to run away. This guy's something of the sort, isn't he?'

'We don't know.'

'Will you have a beer with me?'

'Tomorrow. I need sleep. Call me when you've landed?'

'I promise.'

I close the window before it rains in here too.

GULL SHIT IS NO TRIFLING MATTER

'We've got nothing,' says Stepanovic. He lays one hand next to the other on the table, and he does it with a weight that shows that really he wanted to thump the table – with both hands – but because he knows that obviously won't do any good, he just lays them down.

'We've got Quirin Fuchs, and he's confessed,' I say.

Stepanovic and I are sitting in our cage-squad room; I didn't feel like a table in the murder squad, where I'd have to try not to meet Calabretta's eye. Sahin, Acolatse and Ippig are outside, coordinating with the murder squad to get teams looking for Sebastian Schmidt. So far, this has been a rather haphazard undertaking. We're just combing our way through the entire west of Hamburg. Admittedly, forensics found any amount of evidence that people other than Fuchs and Schmidt had been in the old factory, but that's precisely the problem. It's a massive hodgepodge of trails. Homeless people often sleep in the empty building, teenagers party there, people are going in and out all the time. But in the cellar, there was nothing, except for evidence that Schmidt was tortured a bit by Fuchs; but we knew that anyway. So of course Stepanovic is right. As far as Schmidt goes, we've got sweet FA. Either he got himself free and has gone underground, or someone let him out of the cellar. Our evidence suggests whoever did that could be one of a hundred different people. Either way it's all relatively unsatisfactory.

And this afternoon we've got to face the press. Can't wait. Our press officer is already suitably nervous and has rung twice this morning. He just rang again, actually, but we didn't answer.

'Did you sleep?' I ask.

'Couldn't help it,' he says and yawns. 'Wasn't that bad, actually. I should do it more often. How about you?'

'Couple of hours at any rate.'

'Katsarou's post's been online for an hour or two, by the way. Have you seen it?'

'I haven't,' I say, 'but that'll be why our press guy just tried to ring again. Have you read the story? What's the text like?'

Stepanovic shrugs his shoulders.

'Most likely it's exactly what Quirin Fuchs wanted. His view of the world, passed on unfiltered. It's got nothing to do with serious journalism. His colleagues will come down hard on us this afternoon, and for good reason. If we had an unharmed Sebastian Schmidt up our sleeves, surely it would help to alleviate the whole thing a bit.'

'Perhaps we ought to have a drink or two beforehand to cheer the occasion up at least,' I say, looking at my phone which has just started to ring. 'Wait a moment.'

I answer.

It's not the press spokesman, it's one of the secretaries from the Prosecution Service. The school files have arrived from Nuremberg. I ask her to have them brought over here at once. Then hang up and say: 'We've got the school files.'

Stepanovic runs both hands over his face and breathes a sigh of relief.

'I'll just go out and get us some coffee,' I say.

He nods and gives me a thankful look, which is actually for the fact that something's happening. By the time I get back, we ought to have the school files in front of us – the Public Prosecution Service is based just round the corner.

Outside, it's raining. And it's got cold. Wham, down to twelve degrees. Hamburg in the autumn, and I'll bet there'll be another five months of this.

The bakery next door has a window onto the street from which they sell coffee in paper cups. I join the queue, and just as I take delivery of the two cups, a gull swoops down and craps on my sleeve.

Hey. Between friends? I think. Don't the gulls and I have a good thing going?

The specialist bakery saleswoman seems rather considerate; she hands me a pile of paper napkins, and I try to rescue my trench coat. Gull shit is no trifling matter. I feel as though it could almost hold its own against goose shit. Whatever. The coat's wrecked; it'll have to go to the cleaners. Perhaps I should resurrect my leather jacket. Perhaps I've been making a big deal about that jacket for long enough.

I take the two coffees and head back to Stepanovic.

He's just cracking open the first file; the folder is labelled: 'Biesendorf 1983/84'. I sit beside him and put the coffee down between us.

'And?'

'Here,' he says, leafing through. 'Class five in February 1983. There are Tobias Rösch, Leonhard Bohnsen and Sebastian Schmidt. And, according to the half-yearly report, there's a new pupil: Matthias Nachtweih.' He flicks on through. 'He's put in a room with Rösch, Bohnsen and Schmidt.'

'There he is,' I say. 'Matthias Nachtweih.'

'Or "Schmidt's Cat",' says Stepanovic.

I pull the file for the academic year 1988/89 from the crate on the floor behind Stepanovic's chair, and flick through. It must be here somewhere; they were in year ten…

I don't believe it. I push the file over to Stepanovic, open at the page that shows when exactly Matthias Nachtweih was admitted and to which hospital, and he says: 'Holy shit.'

And of course he's right.

Somebody must have tipped a full flask of coffee over the file. And then wiped it off. Or showered it off. You can just about make out that there was an emergency on the night of the 19th of February and that the emergency had something to do with someone called Matthias. The rest of the page is entirely smudged, not to say destroyed.

'All the same, we've got to look for him,' I say.

'Definitely,' says Stepanovic. 'How long have we got before the press conference?'

The big clock on the wall above our heads says four hours.

'Come on,' I say, 'we'll hunt the name through every computer system we've got.' And we're almost a little excited by it.

After three hours, it's clear that not even the computer systems have the faintest idea of whether or not Matthias Nachtweih is still alive, and, if he is, where he might have got to.

Stepanovic goes to the drawer that holds the forms with which we can apply very formally for official help from Bavaria. He looks pretty depressed about it.

A couple of cops down there will soon have the glorious mission of trudging round every hospital between Würzburg and Nuremburg. Nobody really wants to saddle anyone else with stuff like that.

THE WILD WEST
(STARTS JUST BEYOND HAMBURG)

Press conference in the big hall. They're all there: newspapers, radio, TV, internet magazines. They nail us to the wall.

I say that we've got a confession from the culprit. Stepanovic says that we've got another suspect, although – cough – you couldn't exactly call it 'got', but Stepanovic doesn't say that. So, seen from the outside, we're sitting reasonably pretty.

But, of course, they hate us for the business with Katsarou, as was to be expected. They say we've flouted all the rules and conventions, that we've behaved like we're in the Wild West. And of course we have. Except that everyone currently slagging us off would have given their right arms for Katsarou's story. In the end, they're just mad as hell because they weren't in his position.

We tell them we quite understand that they'd have liked the story themselves.

Then it gets so loud that we don't say anything more at all, and we leave it to the press officer to pull us out of the shit.

AND WHEN ALL THE LANTERNS HAVE BEEN SHOT OUT, YOU'LL REALISE THAT YOU CAN'T EAT FOG

It's not late, but it's already getting dark. It's been raining all day. It's always the same on those days when the light in the sky hasn't come on even once: it just gets dark far too early.

Unless that only happens in my head.

We've just had that exhausting press conference at which I had no better answers than those I actually had, yet everybody felt that I ought to have better ones. I'm just not the type who gives good answers.

I ask myself too many stupid questions for that.

I'm sitting at the window, watching the streetlights come on one after another. I'm drinking a beer and smoking a cigarette.

If we don't find Sebastian Schmidt by tomorrow or the day after, the cage squad will be radically pared down; in other words: disbanded. The search for Matthias Nachtweih will be coordinated from Bavaria, Stepanovic will vanish back to the 44s, Sahin will pick up her job at HQ again, and the only people still trying to find Schmidt will be Ippig and Acolatse, most probably without success. Over the years, quite a few people in Hamburg have simply fallen into the Elbe, slipped under a pontoon and been eaten by the current. And I'll crawl back into my room, in the hope that Dr Kolb will fetch me back out again in good time.

Dazzling prospects.

Perhaps I should just go straight down to the Blue Night and tell Rocco about everything I saw in the Sorgenbrecher yesterday, just to smash all the rest to pieces as well.

Outside, a teenager skates past. The rain has changed into thick fog; it's so quiet in this part of town that the sound of hard rubber wheels on cobbles completely dismantles the street.

Then there's a knock. When there's a knock, it's always Klatsche. I briefly consider pretending I'm not here, but in the end, I know that I can't keep weaselling out of this forever. We need to talk; that's been obvious for days, weeks maybe, or possibly even years. The question is, about what exactly?

I tear myself away from the window, walk to the door and open it. He's standing in the doorframe, but not as come-hither cool as normal, and he's got a leather jacket on. The jacket's zipped up to the top. He really doesn't look as though he wants to come in. He looks more like he's just popped by.

'Have you got a minute?' he asks.

He's just popped by.

'Sure,' I say. 'D'you want to come in?'

He nods, although 'want' is presumably not really the word for it; or at least, that's how it feels. He takes a step towards me and attempts something like a hug. We fail.

'Beer?' I ask, pointing towards the kitchen.

'Nah, don't bother.'

'Cigarette?'

'Yes. I'll have a cigarette.'

We go into the sitting room and sit against the wall, on the floor. I have no furniture, just this old sofa that I lie on once a year. I really must get rid of that soon.

'OK,' I say, lighting two cigarettes and handing him one. 'Who goes first?'

He looks me in the eyes, and there's an unbearable sadness in his gaze. I drag on my cigarette and look away.

'You first,' he says.

I take a swig of my beer and hold the bottle out to him, and he does drink some.

'Something's not right,' I say. 'It's as if we've gone off balance.'

'I've sublet my flat,' he says. 'I'm moving out next week.'

Boom. The sentence lands like a punch between my eyes. It hurts right away. Something rips open in my heart – as big as the San Andreas fault.

But I do look at him again, and now it seems to be him who can't bear my gaze.

He gulps.

'I met a girl in the summer. It was nothing serious.'

A girl. Not a woman. Nothing serious. Right.

'There were a few nights. We were always OK if that kind of thing happened now and then.'

We. The word suddenly seems to be made of hammered steel. How can he say that – 'we'?

He drags on his cigarette and finishes my beer.

'Sorry. Shall I get another from the kitchen?'

I shake my head. Now I want to know what's up. And I say: 'You're moving out because of this girl?'

'She's having my baby. She called me a couple of days ago, then we met up, and that's when she told me.'

'You're going to be a dad?'

I'm amazed that I can ask that question without falling dead on the spot. Klatsche and child. I'd never thought about it. That he might want kids. And obviously all that wouldn't work with me. Because I'm too screwed up, and now I'm also too old.

Now there's a girl, and the girl's having a baby.

'OK,' I say. 'OK.'

'Is that all?' he asks.

I look at him and divert the tears off somewhere. It'd probably be best if I shunted them off into my brain so they could be taken apart there, disassembled into their constituent parts. That'd be good, that'd take the weight out of them, and then they wouldn't fall out of my eyes. So I put all my effort into managing that, and it works. And then I shrug.

Up and back down.

'I've always been waiting,' he says, 'for you finally to say to me: Klatsche, you and me, us, this is the real thing.'

'But we were never like that,' I say.

'Exactly, Chas. We were never like that.'

He stands up.

'I've got to go. Or else I'll start blubbing.'

'OK,' I say.

That's all.

He goes to the door, the door opens, he goes out, the door slams shut. Look at that. It goes as fast as that. And suddenly you're lying on the floor as if you've been run over by a steamroller and you don't know what to do with your remains. I somehow scrape the stuff up; it smells funny. Then I pull myself up onto the couch. At least now I know why I never threw it away.

I go into the kitchen, scraping my knuckles along the wall, against the rough, old plaster. In the fridge, I find half a bottle of vodka, I unscrew it and apply it.

With the bottle at my throat, I'll make it back to my spot on the living-room floor. With the bottle at my throat, the rip in my heart will go away too, piece by piece. But I could swear that for every swig I take, a streetlamp dies out there.

It gets darker and darker.

When the bottle's empty, my phone rings in the distance. Faller, I think, but I can't answer any more.

I DON'T WANT TO SEE THAT

'Is that him?'

Stepanovic leans his head first to the left and then to the right, and looks at what's lying on the ground in front of us.

'Yes,' I say, 'I think that's him.'

Messily run over. The same could be said of my head, but this looks way worse than the massacre in my innards. On the other hand … I'm trying to pull myself together; as for whether I'm succeeding, that's for others to judge, except that they're not looking.

It did start raining again overnight, and apparently it wasn't too stingy about it: the street is soaked to the bones. The water mingles with vast quantities of blood. Somebody ran over Sebastian Schmidt's body more than once. And not just his body. There was a bit of face in there too.

'Oh, my good grief,' I say, and turn away.

I feel sick.

I can hear Stepanovic breathing heavily behind my back. It seems that he can't swallow so much minced meat either.

We're standing on a bridge. To the right are yellow-brick social-housing buildings, probably from the seventies. To our left are elegant office blocks, just the way architects imagined elegant office blocks around the turn of the millennium. The wrought-iron railings and old lampposts are vaguely reminiscent of London two hundred years ago, or come straight out of a fairy tale.

The harbour is straight ahead. Down there, just the other side of the hill, is where Sebastian Schmidt apparently ran over the young woman, a good week ago now. And now he's lying here on the cobblestones, which have definitely seen a lot over the years, but never so much dark, crusty red before.

The mortuary van comes in from the right, feeling its way towards the bridge very slowly and cautiously, as if it didn't want to attract attention. When the van stops and two men in black suits climb out – one about sixty, the other somewhere around thirty – Stepanovic turns to me and says quietly: 'Can't wait to see how they manage to scrape him up off the stones.'

'I can,' I say. 'I don't want to see that.'

'Then look away,' he says. 'But stay with me. I don't actually want to see it either.'

We scan the sky for cranes and try not to listen to what's happening behind us.

'We need to talk to Quirin Fuchs again about Matthias Nachtweih,' I say. 'He's still alive. He's still running around the place somewhere, and he killed Sebastian Schmidt last night.'

'A bold case from the prosecution there.'

'Have you got a better idea?'

'No. But I don't need one. It's nothing to do with me any more. The murder-squad guys are taking over now.'

True. It's nothing to do with me any more either.

'Have you called Calabretta?' I ask.

'Yes, just after I rang you. He ought to be here any minute.'

Below us a bin lorry is driving down the street towards the harbour. When the lorry brakes rather too sharply at a red light, a bag falls onto the street and bursts. The gulls immediately fly in, as they always do when there's rubbish. But the ravens, which sit in the trees all day, waiting for just such a moment, for a bit of stray refuse, aren't going to let the gulls ruin it for them now. They cry out to heaven in their rusty voices and plunge to the ground. And then they're hacking at each other, ravens on gulls, gulls on gulls, they're all screaming at once, and all for a load of mouldy yuck.

Stepanovic holds a cigarette out to me.

'Thanks,' I say, 'but not now. My head's about to explode. But call me this evening. I'll smoke with you then.'

I look at him, and we both know that I've got to go and, behind our backs, Death is rubbing his hands.

HALF JUST TO MAKE SURE AND HALF BECAUSE THAT'S JUST WHAT I'M LIKE

On the Promenade bei der Erholung in St Pauli. Faller always wants to come here. Fine by me. Today Hamburg has hit me like a smack in the face, so I could really do with a bit of recreational promenading, St Pauli style.

We sit side by side on the bench, drinking beer. Below us, the tourists are running riot on the landing stages.

'Come on, have a go,' he says, and looks at me as if it were Christmas.

He wants me to hold this massive shell up to my ear. He's actually brought me one of those tacky shells you can hear the sea in. I mean, walk fifty metres dead ahead and you'll find one – Bridge 8, Kallsen's Souvenirs, eleven euros ninety-nine.

'Faller, that stuff gives me a headache. All you hear is your own stupid blood.'

'This one's different,' he says, leaning back and drinking a sip of beer. 'Ah.'

He's pulled his hat down jauntily over his forehead. He's wearing his trench coat unbuttoned; straining under his white shirt is a considerable belly. After two months in Spain, his face looks like the cover story on a golden-oldies' lifestyle magazine. Tanned and crazily healthy.

'C'mon, my girl. Do you think I'd have brought you tat like that if it wasn't special tat?'

Oh brother. Then I'll just have to hold this monster to my ear.

Uh oh.

I don't hear the swell of the sea.

I hear it smoking.

It sounds like someone drawing in air and puffing it out again.

'It's smoking,' I say.

'It's breathing,' says Faller. 'That's why I bought it for you. So that you'll never forget to breathe. Because that's the trick. Just keep on breathing. But naturally, you hear someone smoking. Just how twisted are you?'

'No more twisted than you, Faller. I learnt it all from you.'

'There's no need to boast.'

Down on the Elbe, a cruise ship passes by, donating its exhaust fumes to the city.

'And are you really through with the case?'

'I don't know,' I say. 'Now it's a homicide, our cage squad has nothing more to do with it. Depends a bit on Dr Kolb – whether I'm still responsible or not.'

'And? Would you like to be?'

'Don't know.' I hold the smoking shell to my ear.

'Come on. You always know things like that.'

'Right, but this time I'm not in the mood for the stupid hunt that'll follow, because I don't think there's anything to hunt. I think it's just the way it is.'

He takes the shell from me and holds it up towards the sky, God knows why.

'There's always something to hunt, Chas.'

'Yes, sure, but only because whatever people like us are hunting has previously been cobbled together by other people. It's all just one big monster factory. The kids of yesterday are the arseholes of today, and the kids of today are the arseholes of tomorrow, and the kids of tomorrow—'

'Yes, yes, all right,' says Faller. 'But if someone's killed a person, they belong in jail. Regardless of whether or not the victim was an arsehole.'

'You're one to talk.'

He squints with one eye and the other stares fixedly at something on the shell or in the sky or in the world.

'I don't know what you mean.'

Sure, I think, and I say: 'There's method in the principle: for one lot to sunbathe, the others have to stand in the shadows and freeze. We all play along. And then stare wide-eyed with astonishment if, now and then, the guys in the shadows come by and shoot down our sun. No arrests, no prosecutions, no sentences will eliminate the principle for good. Give me back the smoking shell.'

He gives me the thing back, links his hands behind his head and lets a whistle out through his lips.

'Anything else?'

'I don't want to work with Calabretta right now.'

'Sorry?'

He sits on the edge of the bench, and turns and looks at me as if I've whacked him one. He pushes his hat back, his belly moves.

'Oh, they're all nuts at the moment,' I say.

'Who?'

The people I call my friends, I think, and I say: 'The others.'

'What do you mean?'

'Calabretta's messing around with Carla, while Rocco's standing around in the Blue Night like a wet blanket,' I say. 'And Klatsche's going to be a dad and he's moving out next week.'

Faller leans back and puffs out his cheeks.

'Oof,' he says. 'Does it hurt?'

'Sometimes,' I say.

'I'm surprised you're not permanently pissed.'

'You didn't see me last night.'

He shakes his head. He's not much of a talker. He puts his arm round my shoulders. We finish our beer. Then he pulls another two bottles from his bag.

'How many have you got in there?' I ask, half just to make sure and half because that's just what I'm like.

Faller says: 'Not enough, I reckon.'

'Well will you come with me later, then? I want to go to a bar.'

'No,' he says. 'A bar stool like that is no more than a Zimmer frame. I really feel too young for that.'

SHADOWRUNNER'S HIGH

The last cage. It's standing in the back of the van. We used the van to take it away. First Fuchs took them away, then he did the things to them, then I helped him to get them out.

You can't do something that big alone.

Not the stuff with the cage.

The thing without the cage worked, but it wasn't small. Everything was huge.

The van, the bridge, the tyres, me.

Now I'm small again. Sitting in front of the cage. Don't know if I ought to get in. I've got razor blades again too. They're not the same ones as before, but they feel exactly the same as they used to. Sharp first, then warm.

Then it goes red.

Then you're dead.

Except: what's the point?

THE LIQUORICE SCHNAPPS IS TERRIFYING, BUT WHAT CAN YOU DO?

We'd only arranged to meet for a cigarette. Then we landed up in this back room. Normally, it's a bicycle workshop. There's the shop at the front with all the snazziest bikes behind barred display windows. Whoever had the idea of transforming the workshop into a salon for one night is a genius, because it all works together. The lamps now have red bulbs in them, there are colourful chains of fairy lights hanging from the ceiling, while the walls are lined with pictures rather than tools. Some are very good and some utter shite, as if everyone in the room has painted one at some point, and lots of them have done so more by mistake. In one corner is an improvised bar made from a couple of beer crates and a board, while in another corner, a stool and a table serve as a DJ booth. A gangling man in a generously checked suit is playing records. There's been music by Bill Callahan playing for half an hour, and it doesn't feel as if anything needs to change any time soon. Behind the bar is a tall and beautiful drag queen with short, platinum-blonde hair. She's wearing a tight silver dress and is opening one beer bottle every second. Apart from beer, there's red wine and liquorice vodka. It says so on the black-board hanging on the wall behind the bar. It also says: out of white wine.

The liquorice schnapps is terrifying, but what can you do?

'Cheers,' says Stepanovic.

'Cheers.'

Down the hatch.

At the far end of the bar, or in front of the window onto the yard, are two people wearing rubber animal heads. A duck and a squirrel. The duck is a woman, the squirrel a man. They're holding hands, and if they can see anything through the masks, I'd say they're looking at each other, and if they can breathe, I'd say they're breathing. At the near end of the bar, two young women have set up a chess board and are playing kamikaze chess. Quick, sometimes clever, sometimes idiotic, always painful.

Some people are dancing. Some are lying on the sofas arranged along the walls, and then sometimes they're lying right on top of each other – perhaps they're even making new people, which isn't necessarily always good news. Stepanovic has taken a seat in a deep armchair next to the DJ and has crossed his long legs. The toes of his ankle boots tap to the beat. Above his head is a picture of a Tuareg, behind whose veiled head a blazing desert sun is sinking below the horizon. He's laid an old newspaper on his lap; lying on the newspaper are a cigarette paper and a small filter. He snaps one of his Luckies and loads the tobacco onto the tiny, thin paper, then he pulls a plastic bag out of his jacket pocket and crumbles marijuana on top of the tobacco.

'What are you doing?' I ask, although I obviously know what he's doing.

'I'm a child of the sixties, why?'

'I'm a child of the seventies,' I say.

'Well then,' he says. 'It fits. And I'd rather have hay fever than a Hollywood cold – wouldn't you?'

I sit on the arm of the chair and watch his construction work. He lights the finished and highly impressive joint and inhales the smoke slowly but thoroughly. After two drags, he hands it to me. Spreading across his face is a peace that I've never seen on him before.

'I haven't done this for years,' I say. 'I don't think I can any more.'

'It's like riding a bike,' he says, 'you never forget. I only started again myself a couple of years ago. It helps with this business of the present, you see.'

I take the joint and drag.

True, I think, ten minutes later. You don't forget. And it does help with this business of the present.

He looks at me and lays his hand on my cheek.

'The later it gets, the more beautiful you become.' Then he comes closer. 'Or is that the weed talking?'

'It's the weed,' I say.

'Yes, that's it,' he says, grinning like a builder. 'Of course you actually look a total mess.'

'Oh, go and do one, Ivo.'

'I'd rather do you.'

I take a deep breath. I probably ought to smack him about now. But then I think – and perhaps it's the dope that makes me think it – you can't choose whether or not you get hurt. But you do have a bit of a say in who by.

I say, 'Budge over,' and I drop into the soft, wide armchair beside him. I lay my head on the back and listen to Bill Callahan, singing stuff that's incomprehensible yet cuts to the heart in equal measure.

We spend time like that and send smoke signals.

Later, when the room regains some of its shape, and Stepanovic is rolling the next joint in order to blur it again, I take my phone in my hand and think about telling everyone what's going on here and ordering them to get down to this back room right away, as a kind of conciliatory gesture. But then I give it a miss, pocket my phone again, stand up and get another two beers.

ACKNOWLEDGEMENTS

My thanks go to:

Karen Sullivan for everything she is, for her support, her love, her laughter, her magnificence.

West Camel for tight but tender editing.

Rachel Ward for the incredible job she does – translating this stuff must be like going through a language hell.

My Team Orenda mates for their open arms and hearts – you are all fantastic.

Nora Mercurio again and again and again.

Alex Glück: without your stories there wouldn't be this story; and Sonja Schäfer, because we're still friends after all this time.

The press office at Hamburg Police for providing the perfect person to talk to.

KDD Kerstin for the tip.

The Kurhaus and everyone in it, for always burning the midnight oil with me; and Johnny for having the right idea at the right moment.

Christian Delles, Matthias Arfmann, Jan Eißfeldt, Dennis Lisk and Guido Weiß, for their unbureaucratic help and generosity.

Werner Löcher-Lawrence, in any situation.

Domenico and Rocco, Romy and Wilhelm: without you all would be nothing.

'Serrated cynicism searing effortlessly through a ghostly city backdrop.
An essential new voice in the genre' Matt Wesolowski, author of Six Stories

BLUE

NIGHT

SIMONE BUCHHOLZ

'If Philip Marlowe and Bernie Gunther had a literary love child, it might just
explain Chastity Riley – Simone Buchholz's tough, acerbic, utterly
engaging central character' William Ryan, author of The Constant Soldier